Cookies and Chaos

A Small Town Culinary Cozy Mystery

Maple Lane Cozy Mysteries
Book 3

C. A. Phipps

This book is for my amazing grandchildren.

Cookies and Chaos

🌑 *A delicious Cozy Mystery with free recipes!*

When Murder comes to town!

Using her bakery and expertise, Madeline Flynn helps the sheriff's twin nephews with their cookie sales—until strange things happen at the community center where they sell them.

With a puzzling death, vandalism and a nasty scam, the danger on their doorstep can't be ignored. Maddie is once again whisked up in an investigation that will take all her sleuthing skills.

Gran, a posse of girlfriends, plus Big Red, her faithful Maine coon, won't let her do it alone. Along with the handsome sheriff, they're wading through clues as thick as cookie dough, hoping that the timer won't go off on another murder.

Have they bitten off more than they can chew?

The Maple Lane Mysteries are light, cozy mysteries featuring a quirky, cat-loving bakery owner who discovers she's a talented amateur sleuth.

Other books in The Maple Lane Mysteries
Sugar and Sliced - The Maple Lane Prequel
Book 1 Apple Pie and Arsenic
Book 2 Bagels and Blackmail
Book 3 Cookies and Chaos
Book 4 Doughnuts and Disaster
Book 5 Eclairs and Extortion
Book 6 Fudge and Frenemies
Book 7 Gingerbread and Gunshots
Book 8 Honey Cake and Homicide - preorder now!

Sign up for my new release mailing list and pick up a free recipe book!

5* "Cookies and Chaos has a solid storyline, however, what makes this so enjoyable for me are the characters. I recommend the entire series." ~ Dorothy S.

Chapter One

Madeline Flynn ignored the ringing phone. Either of her two intern bakers, busy in the kitchen behind her, would answer it. Right now she needed to keep her focus on her VIP customers, ten-year-old twins, Jesse and James Dixon, who were very seriously considering what to choose for their after school treat.

She smirked a little at the idea that whatever he bought them would last that long. Apart from her time living in New York, she'd known the pair for most of their lives and was embarrassed to be unable to tell them apart and had to find a new way each time she saw them to do so. She wasn't alone in this, but it annoyed her ordered mind.

Their uncle, Ethan Tanner, who happened to be the sheriff, gave her an amused wink followed by a shake of the head in mock exasperation as he waited for them to make up their minds.

Their dark hair and blue eyes were so unusual that they required a second look from most people. Those eyes were exactly like their uncle's and weren't the only similarities between the three. The boys had also picked up Ethan's mannerisms, which was natural since he was their only father figure. The way they leaned forward and then back, rocking on the balls of their feet right now, was just one example that made her grin.

Sharing a childhood growing up in the small town of Maple Falls, which was not too far from Portland, Oregon, she and Ethan had some history. It was fair to say that her attention was equally divided between the twins and the handsome sheriff, who looked so darn fine in his uniform that she struggled to refocus on the boys each time he looked her way.

Maddie worked in New York City for a few years but moved back to Maple Falls when her gran created a ruse that she needed help. Soon after her return, she and Ethan had started flirting with the idea of dating again. After hours of deliberations, the main thing holding her back was the risk of losing their rekindled friendship. She'd thought it lost after their bitter break-up years ago.

She also had to acknowledge that the experience of a disastrous relationship during her time in New York City, where her ex had wanted her to be something she wasn't, contributed to her hesitation.

However, their relationship was begging to be given a second chance—like one of her recipes that hadn't quite made the grade on the first attempt. She had missed his friendship so much and was delighted to let it develop. She just wasn't sure it was possible to be romantically involved and still maintain that valued friendship. The attraction was definitely mutual, and thankfully they had both matured from the teenagers who couldn't agree on many things.

"The bakery looks to be doing a roaring trade."

His voice brought her back to the present when Ethan nodded at the full tables of regulars who were devoted to the breakfasts of fresh bagels and croissants she offered.

"It is. I'm having to discourage Gran from increasing her hours again, because Laura, Luke and I are managing well. I might even hire another person to finally get the Saturday opening off the ground."

"As long as you don't have to work any harder."

She grinned at his censure. "Unlike you? How is sheriff work today?"

"All good. I've got some disgruntled Country Club members complaining about someone tearing up the golf course in a van and a suspicious character lurking around town. Just the usual." He winked then turned to his nephews. "Come on, boys. Choosing can't be this hard."

Six-foot-four, with an easy smile, that showcased his dimple, Ethan towered over the boys, who weren't even slightly intimidated by his growly voice.

"But they all look so good. It's tough to decide on just one."

One of them pointed at the display case, while the other nodded enthusiastically.

Maddie proudly straightened her white apron, which was emblazoned with the Maple Lane Bakery logo featuring Big Red, her amazing Maine Coon cat.

"Don't even think about it, James. The last time you two had more than one, you were on a sugar high for hours."

Pushing her long blonde braid over one shoulder she took note and felt pleased that she'd latched on to the fact that James wore a blue cap.

"It's not our fault that Maddie makes them like that," Jesse explained.

"Hey, leave me out of it." She raised both hands. "I don't force you to eat them."

James considered her more carefully, his features thoughtful. "You're a really good baker, but you're kind of like a deputy too now, aren't you? Are you and Uncle Ethan going to solve any more crimes together?"

"Are you undercover?" Jesse added in what was probably supposed to be a whisper.

The blue eyes were innocent, but the memory of what James was referring to, gave her a jolt. Solving the murder of the mayoral candidate last summer and the blackmail around it had been horrible and wonderful in equal measure.

Horrible in that Maude Oliver was killed, arguably by accident, and wonderful that they had saved more than a dozen beloved pets from potential death. The whole thing still made her shudder.

She turned to look through to the back of the shop, where Big Red lay in a pool of sunlight just inside the back door of the industrial kitchen. The massive Maine Coon had been one of the pets that had been stolen for ransom, and she'd been afraid that she would never see him again. He was her best friend and confidante, even before her school friend, Angel, who she'd known nearly as long as Ethan.

Angel owned the hair salon two doors down from Maddie and they saw each other every day, but Big Red hardly left her side ... unless he was chasing butterflies or guarding the back door from unwanted visitors, which may or may not include delivery men. The determination depended on his mood and whether or not he liked whoever dared invade his territory.

"No. I'm a baker. I like to help your uncle if I can, but

I'm not a secret anything."

They looked disappointed, but went back to making their selection, and the moment passed.

Luke, her young intern, came through from the kitchen, looking apologetic and awkward. "Sorry to interrupt, but there's a call. I tried to deal with it, but he insisted on talking to you."

Maddie felt his unease at being left to serve Ethan, but it wasn't something she could prevent indefinitely. The sheriff had grilled the teenager at length in regard to that murder and the blackmail, but there had been no evidence to prove he had anything more to do with it than protecting his brother's girlfriend who had shown signs of abuse.

"I won't be long. Probably not as long as it takes them to choose," she said to Ethan and winked at the twins, who laughed before going back to their selection.

"How are you, Luke?"

"I'm good, thanks."

Maddie smiled at the exchange, hearing the slight stilt-edness in both men as she went into the kitchen. The call was from her supplier, apologizing that their delivery man, Owen, was having vehicle issues and her order wouldn't be delivered until tomorrow. Fortunately, she had a fear of this very thing happening and never let her stock get too low, so it wasn't a problem.

It was odd that this wasn't the first time Owen had problems delivering her order on the right day. He'd started out so efficiently a few months back and had a quick wit that had her interns in fits of laughter. Even Laura, who took time to warm to a person.

Lately, Owen looked exhausted. And kind of sad, although he tried to hide it. You could never tell what was really going on with people, and she didn't feel she knew him well enough to pry.

When she finished, Ethan and Luke were talking quietly, the awkwardness gone. She took the time to frost two butter cookies with clown faces then carried them out to the shop on a tray.

"How about these?" She showed them to the boys and was rewarded with fist pumps.

"Awesome!"

"Cool!

"Thanks for that." Ethan grinned. "Although, you shouldn't spoil them."

"Why not? They're good boys," she answered sincerely.

He looked at the twins, who were arguing over which one they wanted. "Hmmm. I'll take the compliment on behalf of their mother and run."

"Maddie?"

"Yes, Jesse?" She couldn't keep a little pride from creeping into her voice at getting their names straight.

"Ahhh ..."

He seemed to be trying to get the words just right, and his brother gave him a dig with an elbow.

"We want to do some fundraising."

"Good for you." She stole a look at Ethan who seemed just as confused.

James held his cap in his hands, something that his uncle did frequently, and threw her a beatific smile, as if he were trying to get on her good side for a reason she couldn't fathom. He topped it off with an exaggerated sigh.

"Our old bikes are falling apart and they're for babies. We need bigger ones so we can ride to school, and Mom can't afford new ones right now."

Ethan's cheeks pinked. "I'm sure we can work something out," he blustered.

James continued as if he hadn't spoken. "Mom told us not to ask Uncle Ethan for money. She said we have to come up with an idea to help ourselves, so we did."

"That's great. Want to share?" Maddie knew this was a rhetorical question because both boys were bursting to tell her.

They nodded enthusiastically.

"We thought if we made cookies, we could sell them around town," James said, as if he'd won at Ready Player One.

"Sounds like a good plan. What did your mom say about doing that?" she asked, knowing full well that Layla's job and looking after these two filled her days and nights.

"Mom said she doesn't have time to help us bake and we can't use the oven on our own," Jesse confirmed.

Suddenly it all fell into place for her and by the look of Ethan's astonishment he also understood what they were getting at. As much as she wanted to help, Maddie was exhausted by the end of the week and had put her other business plans on hold because of it.

"I see where this is going, guys, but I'm busy myself."

Their faces fell, which made her feel bad. Gran had always made time for her love of baking, despite running a small farm.

"Maybe I could help?"

Luke had been cleaning tables and now he'd stopped, cloth in hand, his offer sincere.

Ethan turned to him. "I don't think my sister would like her home used as a bakery. Plus, she doesn't allow strangers there."

Red-faced at the snub, Luke nodded. "I have spoken to

her a few times, but I hadn't thought about her not really knowing me."

Maddie frowned as she packaged the cookies separately in paper bags and handed them to the boys. They thanked her but were disappointed about the outcome of their request. Their down-turned mouths made the whole thing into a tragedy, and Maddie couldn't let it end this way.

"If I was on site, and Luke baked with them here, would Layla have any objections?"

Surprised, Ethan took a moment to digest the suggestion then raised an eyebrow.

"I guess it's not really my call, but I'll pass along the message to Layla, or perhaps you could discuss it with her?"

"Please, Maddie. Mom won't say no to you." James begged unashamedly, as he and his brother hopped from foot to foot.

"Tell you what, I have to visit the community center this afternoon with Gran, so I'll drop by the clinic while I'm out."

It was like they'd won the lottery, the way they leaped around her. She was even bombarded with several hugs.

Ethan calmly intervened. "All right you two, you're squashing Maddie. She won't be able to plead your case if she can't breathe."

Immediately they stepped back.

"Are you okay?" Jesse asked with concern.

She laughed. "I'm fine."

Ethan wrestled with their bags as he added the cookies to their lunchboxes. It was awkwardly cute.

"This will teach me to bribe them with treats first thing in the morning." He rolled his eyes. "I better get them to school before the principal has my hide."

Maddie laughed again as she watched them go in the

noisy way of boys. The principal was a tiny five feet, two inches and a force to be reckoned with. Suzy Barnes was a friend of theirs and, while she wasn't physically imposing, she had developed other means to keep her pupils, parents, and staff in order, which meant it was rare that anyone was late for school.

Luke returned to his cleaning with gusto and began humming a happy, if unrecognizable, tune.

"That was very kind of you to offer to help them, especially since you don't know them very well."

He ran a hand through his close-cropped fair hair. "I think entrepreneurial kids need to be encouraged. I had so many ideas as a kid, but my dad insisted I get good grades and play football. Nothing else. The grades I managed—football not so much. Anyway, I hadn't intended to use the bakery, but it will be easier with all the pans and the size of the oven. I hope I didn't overstep and force you into offering to let them do it here?"

"Not at all. I would have been happy to help them myself, but I think it's going to take several sessions and even though I'm not ready to open on Saturdays right now, I'm looking at opening up my cooking class to the public."

Currently, Maddie held a class for her friends. It had gone so well and been so much fun she thought it was time to listen to what many of her customers wanted and run one that other members of the community could attend. She'd been mulling it over for months and helping the boys could potentially affect that if she took more of a hands-on role.

Luke's green eyes lit up. "So many people have asked you about it, I don't think you'll have a problem getting people to sign up."

"Thanks for the vote of confidence, but I still have some things to iron out. Back to the twins—if Layla says yes, we'll need to decide how to manage them safely around the oven and sharp utensils."

"Absolutely."

Laura, her other intern came out of the kitchen with a fresh batch of cookies.

"What needs managing safely?" she asked.

Maddie explained, and Laura gasped.

"You're going to let the twins run wild in our lovely kitchen?"

Maddie appreciated it wasn't ideal but thought Laura's horror was a little over the top.

"With Luke organizing and overseeing them, they should be fine."

"I guess it is your kitchen." Laura wasn't convinced.

"Maybe we could say it's a trial. If they don't listen, then we can nip it in the bud."

Laura sighed with relief. "I think that's a wonderful idea. I'd help too, but kids scare me." She looked away in embarrassment and patted her red bun, which had not a hair out of place.

Maddie had a sudden recollection of instances where Laura had been busy elsewhere when the children came in prior to or just after school. Actually, it happened most days.

"You're not serious about them scaring you?"

Laura nodded emphatically. "Very serious, I'm sorry to say. They seem to sense my fear and use it to their advantage."

Maddie had a vision of Laura jammed into a corner with a pack of wild children poking her with sticks.

"That's a shame. Maybe, we should introduce you to them in short bursts? Like an allergy that you build up immunities to."

Luke was fascinated with the interchange and unsure if it was fact or fiction. It was common to have banter in this kitchen—and at Gran's place too—but he was still relatively new to it, so she gave him a wink.

He grinned immediately. "I'll keep them back, Laura, but I would say that watching you frost a cake or putting jelly into doughnuts would have them eating out of your hand."

And, just like that he was one of the team in every sense. Laura was both flattered and speechless.

Maddie smiled. "Well done, Luke. The force is strong in you."

He'd probably heard the Star Wars reference many times but had the decency to laugh. Laura, on the other hand, didn't seem to have a clue as she shook her head and went back to her baking, stopping to give Big Red some loving on the way.

Her fluffy feline arched his back at the head rub. He adored Laura, but would he feel so benevolent towards the boisterous twins?

Chapter Two

When the shop had its late morning quiet spell, Maddie sat Luke down in the small alcove that served as her office adjacent to the kitchen. They began to work out a few things around the cookie-making venture, mostly the safety and hygiene aspects.

"There's no point in going into too much other detail before I speak to Layla. I'll stop by the clinic before the community center."

Luke ran his hands along the edge of the counter. "While we're alone, I want to say again how grateful I am to you for sticking up for me with the police, but also with our customers. I know having your support has helped a great deal with how people in town see me. Instead of judging me by my brother's crimes, as some initially did, plenty of residents have been going out of their way to ask how I am."

Maddie's heart went out to him. The petnapping and murder were horrendous for everyone, but poor Luke had been the scapegoat for his brother. It was particularly annoying when no two siblings had ever been less alike.

"If anything I've done or said has helped, then I'm glad, but I imagine having the sheriff explain things was far more effective than anything I could contribute."

Luke looked up. "I don't know about that; you and Gran have a lot of sway in Maple Falls. Although, I still can't believe he did that for me."

She smiled at his flattery while not entirely agreeing. "Why not? Ethan's a good man, and so are you. You've taken the chance to prove it many times, but I don't think you need to do more than be yourself. And, perhaps staying away from anything that could harm your reputation is good advice."

He nodded. "I will, I promise. Straight after the court case I had the feeling I'd already damaged it beyond repair. I got funny looks, and I overhead whispers and mutterings about my family which aren't true. Mostly. Things are gradually getting better, and I feel like I can start to hold my head up ... around here, anyway."

It was hard to see this nice young man in pain and so unsure of himself. A lot had happened since the day he had dared to go against his father's wishes and train with her—good and bad.

"I'm sorry that you've had to deal with the back lash. It's not fair. Just give the ones who haven't understood a little more time, and they'll appreciate, as the rest of us do, that his crimes have nothing to do with you."

"I hope you're right, and I hope Layla won't say no to the boys baking here because of me."

So that was it—he didn't want to disappoint the boys. One more sign that he was worth helping.

"I'm sure she won't have a problem with it," Maddie reassured him, hoping she was right. Luke did not need another knock to his self-confidence.

They worked hard all morning. After lunch, when the customers dwindled, Maddie loaded up her jeep, affectionally named Honey, with cakes and cookies for the regular Tuesday afternoon tea at the community center.

Other than the bakery, Honey was her pride and joy—a gift from her late grandad after high school graduation. Grandad had taught her everything she needed to know to keep Honey in top condition, and this was her other passion.

It was a shame that she didn't get to take her out much due to the long hours she put in at the bakery, so she was looking forward to the drive, no matter that it was a short one.

Gran would get a ride from Jed Clayton and meet her there with her own contribution. Together with the community center committee, they raised funds for various charities.

"I should be back in time to close up," she told her interns, appreciating how diligent and capable they were to carry on without her around.

She drove to the clinic first, hoping to see Layla and get that out of the way before it bothered her more than it already did, and there was no point in conjecture.

Stubborn like Ethan, Layla was a fantastic mom, and an excellent nurse. Maddie hoped that her nurturing side might help her see that Luke could be another good role-model for the twins.

When Maddie entered the reception area, Layla was bringing a patient out of the doctor's room. She smiled when she saw Maddie and continued to walk the elderly man to the door, talking loudly.

"We'll see you tomorrow to check on that dressing."

Mr. Edgar refused to wear his hearing aid, which

caused everyone to either yell or repeat themselves many times.

"It's not necessary, dear. You did a good job with it today." He held up his bandaged arm.

Layla walked in front of him. "I promise you that it is necessary. If we don't do this regularly, your infection will return. Don't make me come find you," she threatened in the nicest possible way.

"If you say so."

He did not look convinced or worried, and after seeing him outside where Bernie, the town's taxi driver, waited to take him home to the Sunny Days retirement community, Layla sighed as she came back to the empty reception area.

"Men. At any age. The only time they want help is when they're in the hospital or have man flu."

Maddie laughed at Layla's portrayal of the male population of Maple Falls and potentially all men.

"Or they want new bikes." It seemed an appropriate segue into the reason she was here.

Layla grimaced. "You've heard about that?"

"I have indeed. And I have the solution."

Layla clutched her heart dramatically. "I'm not sure I want to hear this. What have my terrors conned you into?"

Maddie laughed. "They want to bake cookies to sell. Using my bakery to do it so you don't have to be there."

Layla's look darkened. "They asked to cook in your bakery? I'm sorry, Maddie. They had no right. Wait until I get hold of them."

Maddie put up her hands. "Before you lynch them, let me say that it wasn't their idea to use my kitchen, but I'm happy to let them. The only potential issue is that I don't have a lot of free time, so Luke has kindly offered to watch over them and teach them how to bake cookies."

Layla's eyes widened. "Luke Chisholm?"

"My intern. Yes." Maddie crossed her fingers at her side.

Layla frowned. "This is a huge imposition for someone I barely know."

"The boys like him. He's nothing like his brother if that's what's bothering you." Maddie felt the need to point out.

"Not as much as it probably should. I heard about how he protected Angel's assistant, Beth, so I'm not worried he'll drag the boys into a life of crime. Although, with those two, it would be hard to know who would be leading whom," she added with a touch of irony.

"What's the problem then?"

"Don't you think it's odd for a teenager to want to give up his time this way?"

Maddie grinned. "When you get to know Luke better, you'll see that he loves to help out. Frankly, he loves to bake so much, I don't think he sees it as wasted time."

Layla mulled that over for a few moments. "Your opinion does matter, but what about ingredients and all the mess?"

Maddie obviously had a few qualms around the survival of her pristine kitchen, but she wasn't about to let Layla know about them.

"Luke and I discussed this, and with the boys' agreement, I'll provide the ingredients, then they can pay for them at cost once they sell the cookies. The bonus is that they'll get an appreciation for gross and net profit." She grinned. "And rest assured that the mess will be dealt with by those who make it," she ended firmly.

"Good luck with that." Layla gave a short laugh.

"Where will they sell the cookies? I don't like the idea of them going door-to-door."

"At the community center. I also thought that we could ask Angel and Isaac to sell some on their behalf at the salon and the diner."

Layla gave her a searching look, then nodded. "I can see that you've thought this through. Against my better judgment, I'm going to agree. Please know you can pull the plug if it gets too much, or they don't behave. I won't be offended. I just hope you don't live to regret this."

Maddie smiled, despite the sinking feeling that if even the boy's mom thought this could turn bad, it didn't bode well.

"I will, but I think they'll be fine. And thanks for not holding Luke's brother against him."

"Hey, at some stage we've all needed a second chance." She gave Maddie a pointed look.

Layla had never said anything directly, but clearly she thought Maddie and Ethan should cement their relationship.

With the town having made up its mind and a lot of residents feeling the need to comment, she wondered if that was another reason she was so reluctant to commit to Ethan.

Layla's next patient arrived and promising to finalize things and let her know the details, Maddie headed to the community center to begin phase two of her plan.

Some of the people there she could count on, but how would the rest of the group of mostly Sunny Days retirement community residents feel about helping the twins?

Chapter Three

When Maddie arrived at the community center, Gran was already there, having been picked up by Jed Clayton since she didn't drive. This carpooling had begun several weeks back when Maddie was busy managing the bakery on her own and didn't have time to drive her.

Since hiring Laura and Luke, she did have a little more time, and Maddie began to help at the community center as well, which meant, since they were living just down the road from each other, she could have brought Gran. She'd offered but had been turned down.

Until today she hadn't given it much thought. Was there something going on with Gran and Jed? Maddie shook her head at the idea. The two of them had been friends forever which is why they spent so much time together. Simple as that.

She took the food into the kitchen where Gran and her friend Mavis Anderson were making tea and coffee.

"These look delicious," Mavis gushed as she took the

tray and began to put the cakes and cookies onto plates. "Adding these to your gran's blueberry tarts will ensure afternoon tea is another doozy."

The group had wholeheartedly adopted Gran's love of an English afternoon tea. It served a dual purpose of getting everyone together who would otherwise be likely to spend most days on their own and as a fund-raiser for different projects within the community.

Mavis, a round ball of anticipation, was partial to a daily dose of gossip, taken and given with a lighthearted view of life. She lived in the retirement community and knew everyone and everything that happened in and around it. Possibly the whole town as well.

The community center was her other source of information and she was quivering with unasked questions. Right now, it was Maddie's turn.

"How are you doing, dear? I was so proud of you, solving that murder and saving all those pets last summer, but I do worry about the danger you put yourself in when you get involved in other people's dramas."

Gran snorted at the irony, causing Maddie to turn away to hide her grin, although there had been nothing funny at the time. Plus, Mavis had seen her since the petnapping incident and said the same thing each time, almost verbatim.

It was a common thread around town that if you wanted a thing known, tell Mavis. If you wanted a secret kept, tell Gran.

"Having Big Red go missing involved me. I couldn't sit by and wait for him to come home, and Mr. Clayton was losing hope he'd ever get Sissy back."

"Well, I grant you that Big Red is a special cat, and Sissy

is a sweet Labradoodle, but surely the sheriff and his wonderful team could have solved the case without you?"

Maddie gave a non-committal reply. Ethan had worked hard on the case, and she was certainly no substitute for a deputy, but she liked to think she had added a different perspective. Being raised by Gran, who believed in family being a global village, Maddie also had an innate desire to help people and had surrounded herself with like-minded women, affectionately known as the Girlz.

Maddie, Angel, Suzy, and Laura. The first three had been through school together. Laura was a recent addition, but was no less one of them and becoming more so with the passing months since they had known her.

"Shall we take out the refreshments, Mavis?" Gran intervened.

"My, yes. Everyone has paid their five dollars for the fundraiser."

Once a month, the community center committee of which Gran was still the president, raised money for different charities and groups in the area. Today it was for play equipment at the local nursery school.

The large room was sectioned into two by a couple of sliding screens, so it could be used by more than one group at a time. When they went through into their section with plates and cups the area was full of people. It made Maddie proud to see the level of enthusiasm for such a good cause.

Initially she'd seen donating baked goods as a great way to try out new recipes on more than her employees, even though there was the potential for fewer sales at the bakery. She was pleasantly surprised to find that the group was now a source of advertising, since they told all their friends and family.

"What delicious treats are we in store for? Whatever it

is, I know it will be wonderful." Jed Clayton rubbed his hands together.

He was friendly to Maddie before, but since he'd gotten Sissy back, he couldn't say enough kind things to and about her. The group erupted at his words trying to see past them to see what was on the plates and made guesses at flavors.

"Today, we have a mini chocolate croissant, chocolate chip cookies, and Gran's blueberry tart."

"Did you hear that?" Jed called out to the others who nodded enthusiastically and settled themselves for Mavis to bring the plates around.

"Take one of each and if there's any left, we'll see." She used her best mothering voice.

Gran handed out cups of tea and coffee, knowing precisely how each person took theirs. Maddie knew she would have preferred to use her own cups, saucers, and plates and was not happy about the community center's set, which were beyond drab in comparison to the ones she had at home and the many others she had donated to Maddie's bakery.

Brought to America as a small child by her English parents, Gran was a lover of everything British, and possessed many coronation, wedding and other kinds of souvenirs.

After they were served, Maddie had the chance to watch their reactions to the cookies and cakes. It couldn't have been better, and she sipped her tea in satisfaction.

"These are your best yet."

"Thanks, Jed."

While it was good to hear, everything he tried of hers was apparently better than the last, so perhaps he wasn't the best person to ask for an honest review.

As they ate, the group branched out from discussing the

food and their latest malaise, to what was happening around Maple Falls.

"Irene Fitzgibbons is handling the mayor's position quite well, isn't she?" Mavis threw out into the group.

"She is indeed, poor woman. It's not like she actually intended to become mayor, but when Mickey Findlay was apprehended, that left her to hold the fort, as it were," Jed added.

It was well known that the Country Club and the Community Center group were often at loggerheads. Yet, since the last disaster over another election campaign mired in controversy, the town was less inclined to be as separate as they once were.

Maddie couldn't have been happier by this outcome. According to Gran, there had never been such separatism when she was young, but the Country Club had only been around for thirty years or so.

Now that Maple Falls was known as the perfect place to retire, since it wasn't too far from Destiny, and therefore, Portland, many wealthy people had arrived to call it home.

"Are all the animals doing okay after their petnapping ordeal?" Mavis asked Jed.

"I've been in touch with some of the owners, and they seem as right as rain. My Sissy has a new lease on life. It took her days to go out by the gate, but I'm not unhappy about that."

Most of the pets had gone missing in broad daylight and owners and pets alike were still wary of it happening again, despite the fact the perpetrator was languishing in jail. Jed kept in touch with some of the owners, who had all been traumatized over losing their pets and being powerless for some time to find out what had happened or how to get them back. It was a sweet outcome that a bond with pet lovers in and around Maple Falls was formed.

"I hope that Owen managed to get his van fixed."

Maddie looked up from her tea at the sudden shift in conversation from Gran's friend. "What do you mean, Mavis?"

"His van has been parked in the back of the retirement community carpark all day. I popped out to ask if he needed assistance, but he said he was waiting for a part."

"That must be the reason for his delayed delivery this morning. I sure hope he can get it here tomorrow."

She said this as an aside to Gran, but Mavis had the hearing of a moth along with its inability to sit still.

"Would you like me to check on that for you when I get home?" she offered.

"No, thanks. I spoke to him earlier and I'm sure it will be fine. You could help with something else, though, if you don't mind?" Maddie raised her eyebrows inquiringly and, anticipating the eager response, had to suppress a smile.

"Certainly, dear." Mavis began to quiver again.

"I believe all the committee members are here. I wonder if I could have a word with them about having another afternoon tea, but on Saturday afternoons? Just for a few weeks."

Mavis clapped her hands to silence the group. "Maddie has a request for the committee, but I'm sure we can deal with it here. We're all friends, after all."

There was a mixed reaction, to which Mavis was oblivious. It wasn't usual to have requests made so openly and some were sticklers for protocol. Maddie hadn't had a chance to brief Gran either. Fortunately, their shorthand came into play in moments like this.

"Is it for a special fundraising event?" Gran asked, innocently.

Maddie's answer was pitched for all to hear. "Very special. Layla Dixon's boys need new bikes and they have to find the money themselves. If they could sell cookies every week, on Saturdays, I'm sure they could achieve it."

"We only do the teas for charity. I don't see how kids' bikes qualify." Nora Beatty, the Debbie Downer of this lively group, spoke up.

As Gran replenished her cup, she spoke gently. "Now, Nora, isn't it true that charity begins at home? These boys are without a father. Layla works hard, but it must be financially difficult to bring up two growing lads on her own."

"Think about all the lessons they could learn from this: Working hard gets you what you want. Math - with the money side of things. And learning how to bake wouldn't be a bad thing for a boy. Look at poor Jed. He's a hopeless cook, and he's not the only man I know who can't fend for themselves and could have benefited from a few lessons," Mavis concluded.

Jed's mouth opened and closed a few times, but in the end he remained silent.

"Little boys are always dirty," Nora intoned.

Unfortunately, this received several nods from the group.

Maddie sniffed. "I can assure you, since they'll be making their cookies at Maple Lane Bakery, all standards of hygiene will be addressed."

"You'll be making the cookies with them?" Mavis asked, excited as a hummingbird.

Maddie got the feeling that the project might stand a better chance if she was the one teaching the twins, but she wouldn't lie about it. "No. The boys will make them, overseen by Luke, my intern. He's an exceptional student and I have complete faith in him."

Nora tutted. "Wasn't his brother involved in the petnapping?"

Gran intervened before Maddie could react.

"Yes, but Luke helped to solve the mystery and return the animals. We can't pick our families, can we?"

Some of the residents from the retirement community, including Nora, had family, yet hardly had a visitor between them. Nora understood the reference and was quiet. The others also reflected on this while Gran smiled sweetly at Nora to take the sting out of her words.

"But we can pick our friends, and here we all are having such a grand time. Wouldn't it be great to have another opportunity to do so every week for a while? Plus, it would be a great community gesture to help the boys. Who knows? It may benefit the whole town if they have some constructive way to release all that energy." Gran laughed at her own joke.

"If they don't run us over on faster, bigger, bikes than they already have," Nora added.

Jed rolled his eyes, and possibly in an attempt to thwart an argument Gran offered him another cookie. "I'm sure they'll be well prepared for riding around town and obeying the rules if their uncle has anything to do with it. Shall we vote? All those who agree to Jesse and James Dixon selling cookies here on Saturday afternoons for a few weeks, say 'aye'."

It was a narrow margin, but the vote was carried, and Maddie, feeling her own laughter bubbling up inside her, thought she should quit while she was ahead. She offered the plate of treats to Nora, smiling as big as she knew how.

"Thank you all so much. I'll let Layla know."

Mavis gave her an innocent look. "And the sheriff. He is the boy's uncle, and you two are such lovely friends."

There was a world of innuendo in that remark, and it was reflected in the faces of the rest of the group. It seemed that she and Ethan were already an item no matter what the parties involved thought. Maddie couldn't help a sigh.

"Thank you. I'll let him know too."

Chapter Four

With the kitchen finally clean at the center, Gran was happy to stay a little longer with her friends and get a ride home with Jed, so Maddie took her plates and left.

As luck would have it, she didn't have to look far to find Ethan. He was at the park just across the road from her bakery. She parked Honey in her small garage and went to tell him the good news.

Crouched low, hat in his hand, he was studying tire tracks that definitely weren't from the riding mower that Bernard Davis used. Keeping the town looking neat as a pin was Bernie's passion, although he also loved chatting with his passengers as the local taxi driver.

"Bernie won't be too happy about that."

Unsurprised by her appearance, he glanced over his shoulder and gave her his dimpled smile before standing and replacing his hat. The sheriff towered over her five feet, six inches, blocking the fall sun when she looked up at him.

"He was the one who told me about it. And no, he's not amused. Looks like a van was taking a joy ride."

She bent over the marks to see what he saw. "How can you tell what type of vehicle it was?"

He pointed at the marks. "The width of the tires, and how deep they've sunk into the grass. It must have had a considerable load in it."

He spoke to her as he would one of his deputies and a trickle of pleasure ran through her. Was that weird?

"They've driven over the path there and come back the same way but on a slightly different trajectory." He pointed.

"Then they've headed across the park. Why would they want to do that?" she asked.

He shrugged. "That's the second question."

She tapped her thigh. "The first is where were they going?"

He gave her an appraising look. "Exactly. If we can figure out the where, we'll eventually get to the why."

She stood up, unable to hide her excited and hopeful tone. "We?"

"I meant 'we' as in the department."

She screwed up her nose at his smirk. "Sure, you did."

"Maddie." Ethan warned in his growly voice, which resembled more of a teddy bear than anything scary.

"What? It's not a murder, is it?" she asked, innocently.

"Definitely not," he said, but without conviction.

Having known the sheriff since they were children, she knew when he was worried. "Did something else happen?"

"I don't know what you mean."

She ignored his terrible attempt at outrage. "What was it? More tire tracks? Another vehicle? Maybe a crash?"

"Calm down." He sighed, looking around, then pulled her close. "Since there won't be any peace any other way, I'll tell you what I know."

She tapped her fingers on her thigh again, which made

him raise an eyebrow, so she clasped her hands together. He released her, crossing his arms over his chest before continuing.

"That complaint I told you about, the one where a van has been driving over the country club golf course? I haven't been to check it out yet, so I don't know what damage has been done, but I wonder if the two are related."

"Why would they be?"

He grinned at her feigned casualness, which may have been a little over the top.

"I mean, it might have been the groundskeeper there, or one of the crowd who frequent it. Who told you about it?"

He nodded. "I considered the groundskeeper, but he's new I believe. Anyway, Irene Fitzgibbons called me. She's on the committee, and said he knows nothing about it."

"We were just talking about her at the community center. Everyone thinks she's doing well, especially considering she never wanted the job of mayor."

He gave her a rueful smile. "You know, I feel like she's been given a chance to make a difference, and she's grabbed it with both hands—determined to do so, despite her earlier protestations."

Maddie smiled. Sometimes he might need to be staunch and cool, but he loved Maple Falls as much as she did. He proved it in the way he was always fair to everyone. Even those that had, at times, been very hard work.

Ethan was also patient with her when it came to her curiosity about his job, which she was grateful for. She hoped it was more to do with her different approach to things, but it may have something to do with them flirting with the idea of dating. Flirting, at nearly thirty years old, was proving to be more fun than she would have imagined.

"It does look that way. It must have given her a boost to

have a unanimous vote, and her fears of not being able to cope are proving unfounded. Is she still vice president of the Country Club?"

He grinned. "Acting President for now. She's waiting to see if she can do both jobs without compromising anything."

He headed along the tire marks, and unasked, Maddie walked beside him. It was nice to be out in the colors of fall. Deep-reds, burnt-orange and browns of every hue surrounded them. Hardy leaves clung to trees while others had made their escape and created a carpet that crunched under their shoes.

Big Red, whose hearing could rival Mavis's, came scampering across the road and, after a reproachful look at Maddie for not telling him she was home, he wrapped himself around Ethan's legs.

"Looks like I have more company." The sheriff dutifully bent to give him a scratch on the head before setting off again. His entourage followed with keen interest.

The woods went away to the left and on the right, the bank sloped down to a small stream. Slightly swollen with recent rain it babbled joyously over the small rocks on its way to the lake. This was one of her favorite walks, which she took most afternoons, usually accompanied by Big Red.

They followed the tracks which cut back to the left and went around the wood and out to the main road via a small service area between the stores.

"Looks like they wanted a scenic tour."

"Maybe." Ethan pointed to a slab of concrete between two buildings. "Look at those oil marks. Whoever was driving, parked here for some time."

Maddie bent to study the smears. "How can you tell?"

"There was no leakage anywhere on the way, was there?" He gave her a side glance.

"I wasn't taking too much notice, but I don't recall seeing any. Would it show on the grass?"

"If there was enough of it. I was looking, and there was none. It means there was a gradual leak rather than a hole." He also bent down and picked up a cigarette butt with a plastic bag he removed from his shirt pocket. "Hmmm. This is a pretty standard brand."

He held it out to her, and she took a closer look. "Will you ask around who smokes that brand?"

He nodded. "I will, but the likelihood that anyone can remember the brand people smoke is slim."

She walked carefully along the wall and crouched low. "Ethan, look at this. Someone stood here for much longer." There were at least ten cigarette butts in a pile.

"Good spotting. See the way the butts have been ground into the concrete? Whoever did that will have the same black marks on their shoes. Provided they didn't walk through a puddle, grass, or clean them in some other way."

He was crouched down beside her, his breath tickling her neck as he pointed to the smears. She gave a little shiver, cold in the shadow of the buildings. *Or is it from something else? Why would someone clean their shoes unless they had something to hide?*

Ethan stood and walked to the edge of the building, taking a moment to look up and down the street. "Whoever was in the van, they were waiting here for a reason."

Maddie could see he was thinking aloud, but she had a million questions. "Now we just need to figure out who that was, right?"

He grinned. "You always make it sound so easy."

She gave him an apologetic smile. "I'm sure it's not. I guess I'm trying to figure out your process."

"For future investigations that shouldn't concern you?" he teased.

"It's fascinating. And I like watching you work." She blushed a little, but it was the truth.

"Why, thank you. Flattery will get you almost everywhere. Now, back to why we're here. Feel like a browse?"

On their left was the gallery, which showcased local art and crafts. When she had the chance, Maddie loved looking around inside, but most of the paintings or sculptures weren't cheap. On the right was an appliance and furniture store. Both were open.

"Seriously? I haven't had one of those for ages, you might never get me out of either one."

He laughed. "Then we should start with one and see if we can squeeze in the other before closing."

"Speaking of which, I should get back to the bakery before then. I've been gone most of the afternoon."

"I can do this on my own if you need to go."

He was sincere, but Maddie thought she heard a little wistfulness in his voice, which could be wishful thinking, but the idea made her happy.

"I know that, but ... I guess Laura and Luke can manage without me." She sent off a quick text and followed him inside the gallery.

Chapter Five

"**S**heriff! And Maddie!" Cora Barnes, the diminutive owner, called out from behind a counter which housed jewelry.

Cora was also the mother of Maddie's good friend, Suzy. As much as mother and daughter might look alike, they were as different as a scone and a bagel. Sure, Suzy was a dynamic principal and Cora a dynamic Gallery owner, but that was where the similarity of personality ceased.

Cora wore kaftans. Suzy suits. Cora had embraced the art world and some of its more eclectic members. Suzy preferred a more linear approach to life.

The place was beautifully laid out, with paintings hung to make full use of the expert lighting which had been recently installed. There were also sculptures and other craft work on display.

Maddie would have loved to purchase some of the wonderful paintings, although, not all were her cup of tea.

"To what do I owe the pleasure?" Cora dropped a kiss on Maddie's cheek

"We're just browsing," Ethan said.

Cora beamed. "How wonderful. Does this mean that you two are looking at setting up house together?"

Ethan gave her a wry grin. "That might be a little premature, Cora. I'm still waiting on a first date."

Cora put her hand to her throat in horror. "Goodness, what's the hold-up?"

She directed the question to Maddie, who coughed.

"We've both been swamped."

Cora tutted. "Well, that's no excuse. You two belong together. Everybody knows that."

"Do they?" Ethan grinned, raising an eyebrow at Maddie.

She pressed her lips together for a moment, trying not to laugh. Gran and the Girlz would agree wholeheartedly with Cora, along with plenty of others, but Maddie wasn't going to let anyone pressure her.

She changed the subject. "How's business these days?"

Ethan's grin disappeared at the rogue question, and he turned to listen to Cora's answer.

"Quite steady. Some days I have only a few customers and other times they come one after the other. I prefer the latter, but that's business, isn't it?"

He nodded. "So, I hear. Do you get many out-of-town customers?"

Cora frowned. "Is this a survey? If it is, I have to tell you that I had someone else ask me these very questions a few weeks ago."

Ethan's interest spiked along with Maddie's, but he managed to beat her to the next question.

"Who was it that wanted to know?"

Cora put an orange painted fingernail to her chin. "He was a big man. Nearly as tall as you, Ethan. Gray hair from what I could see, although he wore a cap so he might have been bald. Maybe a little older than Dan. He wore jeans and a shirt, which could have both used a press," she said, as if this was a crime.

Maddie grinned. Cora's husband, Daniel Barnes would not be let out of the house in such a state. "Those are good observations."

"I'm an artist. Trained to notice the small things, you might say," Cora said with pride, as she opened her arms to encompass her beautiful gallery.

"Anything else?" Ethan pressed.

"He had a small scar over his right eyebrow, which gave him a slightly sinister look. That, coupled with the fact that he'd been hanging about in the parking space next door, was a little unnerving. Although, there have been a couple of people doing that lately, so I didn't feel like I could single him out." She shrugged. "I might not like it, but any customer is a good one and when he did come in, he was friendly enough. He actually bought a couple of paintings of mine." She flushed with pleasure.

"Congratulations." Maddie knew through Suzy that Cora didn't paint as much as she used to and that her paintings had never sold particularly well, so any sale was cause for celebration.

"Thank you, dear. I was so excited, and it has inspired me to paint again. Finding the time has been difficult, what with working here alone. But now that Dan has decided to follow the Oregon Ducks so closely, I suppose I'll have a few more hours to spare on the weekends."

Her mouth turned down and she looked away as if she were sad at the prospect, which didn't seem to fit with what she was saying about being happy to be able to paint again.

Ethan didn't seem to notice. "Can I assume that you didn't catch the name of this man?"

"No, it never came up." Cora looked surprised by her own admission. "You know, that is odd. I always find out people's names so that I can speak more familiarly with them. It's a trick I picked up at a sales conference many years ago."

Ethan smiled warmly. "Don't worry about it. Did he pay by cash or card?"

She didn't hesitate. "Cash. Both times."

"Is that usual?"

"Not these days, unless it's something small. Or, I should say, not very expensive. Most people pay by some sort of card, which is probably why I remember he didn't."

"That's a shame. It would have been an easy way to locate him," Ethan mused.

Cora tidied an already straight pile of tissue paper on the counter. "Is this man in trouble?"

Ethan was instantly wary and watched Cora closely. "I'd like to talk to him about a couple of things. That's all."

"That's good. Even though I don't know him well, I'd hate to think he'd done something wrong."

Maddie patted her arm. "I'm sure there's nothing for you to worry about. Ethan and I were out and about when he thought he would come in to say hi and ask about this man."

That made Cora smile again. "Perhaps 'this' could be your first date."

Ethan snorted, wishing her a good day as he walked outside, and Maddie shook her head as she followed. Small towns! Everyone had an opinion, and they weren't afraid to share it.

"So, what do you think that was all about?"

"I have no idea, but I don't like the fact that people are hanging around the shops, even if some of them do buy the odd thing. I'm going to call into the appliance store while we're here. Do you have time to come along?"

She looked at her watch. "Sure. It's nearly closing time, and Laura texted back that she'll lock up for me."

Knowing he didn't need her to come, she was pleased Ethan had asked, and he looked happy that she'd said yes.

Christopher Henderson was serving Mavis when they entered.

"Look, it's the sheriff ... with his girlfriend." She sighed as if they were in some romantic scene from Pride and Prejudice.

"I have some specials if you two are looking at setting up house together." Chris looked at them knowingly.

Maddie had to grit her teeth for a moment, so her smile was perhaps a little less than convincing. *Did Cora phone ahead?*

"I have all the appliances I need, thanks. Remember I bought all new ones for the bakery?"

"Well, sure, but maybe you're thinking of moving into the sheriff's house? I bet he hasn't had a new anything for years. You can't use your industrial ones there, can you?"

Maddie's mouth gaped, and Ethan shuffled his feet.

"Where does everyone get the idea from that we're ready for stuff like this?" he asked to the shop in general.

Mavis bent her head. "It might be my fault, Sheriff. Seeing you two together most days at the bakery, I felt certain you'd be announcing it any day."

"Mrs. Anderson, Maddie and I have just got back together. Any assumptions about the future of our relationship would be premature at this stage, even for us."

She bowed her head. "I'm sorry if I've upset either of you. I let my mouth run away from me sometimes."

Maddie hated to see Mavis so upset. "No harm done.

41

But if you could spread the word that we're only just girlfriend and boyfriend, that might help." She gave Ethan a quick look and he nodded.

"Of course, dear. I'll get on that right away."

She scurried out the door before Maddie could say that it could wait for a convenient time.

Chris roared with laughter. "I hope you don't think it was a fix, telling her that?"

Ethan grimaced. "I know. It'll be a patch at best."

"Her heart is in the right place," Maddie insisted, not sure whether all this was quite as hilarious as Chris seemed to think.

"She does indeed. It's not her heart that gets her into trouble, though. Is it?"

Ethan headed Chris off mid-another-laugh. "Speaking of trouble, I want to ask you about the van that's been noticed parked outside between your store and the gallery on a regular basis."

Chris frowned. "Darn annoying, when I have a delivery, but other than that I haven't had any trouble. Why do you ask?"

"People have commented on it being there for long periods of time. I was checking that no one had any experience with odd behavior or anything else?"

Chris raised an eyebrow. "Like theft?"

"Yes," Ethan said then waited for further comment.

"Not me. I went to check on the van a few times. I wasn't always sure it was the same man driving it. The last time I did, I mentioned to him that he was leaving oil stains on the concrete and Cora and I would appreciate if he either didn't park there or got it fixed. He apologized right away. Said it was a quiet place to read the paper in between dropping off his deliveries, but he could do that elsewhere if we really objected. Ever since that day, I tell him when my deliveries are expected, and he moves on. Can't expect fairer than that, especially after he purchased a couple of small items."

Maddie could almost see Ethan's mind ticking over the ramifications of this. Hers certainly was. To anyone looking at the facts, the man who hung around both stores was innocent of any crimes. He was pleasant and helpful, had spent money at both stores. Only, was it the same man and same white van?

"What did this man look like?" she asked.

"Tall. He wore a baseball cap and had a scar over his right eye."

Snap! It sounded like the same guy Cora had mentioned. Maybe she was wrong about there being two.

"Did you get his license plate number?"

Chris rubbed his chin. "Can't say it occurred to me."

"You said wore. You haven't seen him in a while?" Maddie continued since Ethan didn't seem to mind.

"I couldn't pinpoint the last day I spoke to him, but I think it was last week sometime. He said he was working out of town for a while. Say, are you two working together again?"

"Maddie is here purely by chance." Ethan followed this up with a raised eyebrow to her and she figured she must have said enough for now. "Did he say where he was working?" he asked.

Chris shook his head. "No. He wasn't what you'd call chatty."

"Well, he doesn't sound like he's a threat to anyone, but if you do hear from him or see him will you give me a call? I just want to ask him a few questions."

"Will do, Sheriff."

When they got outside, Maddie turned to ask him what he thought about the whole situation, but he stopped her.

"Not here. Let's get back to my car."

They retraced their steps between the stores and through the park, and to her pleasure Ethan took her hand as they skirted the wood.

Suddenly, from behind a tree a blur of pale red shot out and tackled Ethan around the ankle. He grunted as he tripped, fell forward onto his knees and glared at the felon.

"Big Red! Leave Ethan alone. You know he's our friend."

Her cat sat back, licked his paw with narrowed eyes focused on the fallen sheriff, who clambered to his feet, dusting off his uniform and returning the look.

"I believe that cat is jealous of me."

"He loves you."

"Not lately. Every time I'm near you, he gives me the evil eye."

Maddie would have argued further because she loved her opinionated cat, but the truth was there for all to see. Big Red was her protector and was taking it a little too far.

"Maybe he thinks—you know, with the handholding— that you could hurt me?"

"That sort of protectiveness would be cute, but it's not helping our romance."

They continued back to his car, and she took it upon herself to keep an eye on her wily pet so that Ethan could return to his thoughts without getting knocked down again. And ... they did not hold hands.

When they were standing beside his car and opposite the bakery, Big Red crossed the road and waited on the curb like a father waiting for his daughter after a date. Well, she was not rushing home, so he would just have to sit there.

She had more questions, and she might just burst if she didn't get one or two out of her head.

"What do you really think this is about?"

Ethan's mouth twitched. "I think there are other issues that need my attention more than a stranger who isn't doing any harm. I'll alert my deputies. If we suspect he's causing any trouble, then we can do more to trace him."

Maddie could see his point, although she had an odd feeling about this. But she had to admit that she'd enjoyed her time with Ethan, and that made her smile.

"Well, if nothing else, it was interesting working with you today, Sheriff. Now I'd better get back to the bakery and do some paperwork."

Ethan casually looked up and down the street then pulled her into his arms.

"I'm glad I could entertain you, and I've wanted to do this ever since you arrived on the scene. Now that your minder is across the road, I finally can."

He bent down and kissed her. Her eyelids fluttered closed. Slow and gentle at first, his hand slid to the back of her neck and pulled her against him as the kiss deepened. He was a great kisser and her knees went weak.

A whistle pulled them apart like a sharp knife on a loaf of bread. She staggered a little, forcing Ethan to hold on until she was steady.

The culprits, Jesse and James, ran towards them laughing and pushing each other.

"You guys are gross," one told them.

"So gross," the other echoed.

"Charming." Maddie couldn't prevent a grin.

Ethan wasn't quite so enamored with his nephews. "That's quite enough from you two. What are you doing here, James?"

Of course! That's James. He has the blue cap.

"We've been to the library and have to meet Mom at the clinic. She wants to do some shopping and we have to go too." James grimaced, while Jesse groaned. Then their faces lit up and they nudged each other.

"Could we come with you instead?" James pleaded.

"I can feel a con coming on," Ethan replied.

Jesse threw a little sugar into the mix. "We'd behave. You can show us the cells again."

"And the bad guys." Excited by the prospect, James bounced up and down on the spot.

"We don't have anyone in the cells, but maybe it would be a good place to keep you guys for an hour or two. I'll ring your mom."

The boys gave each other high fives at his easy capitulation, as if they'd planned this prior to them meeting. Knowing these two, it wasn't out of the question.

"You won't really put them in the cells, will you?" Maddie whispered as he slipped his phone from his pants pocket and pulled up Layla's number.

"Sure." He grinned. "But I won't lock the door, if that makes you feel better?"

He was laughing at her, and she didn't mind. "I guess if their mother doesn't mind it must be okay. I'll see you later."

"Count on it." He winked as he opened the back of his sedan to let the boys file in with their school bags, chattering about bad guys and clearly delighted with themselves.

She watched him finish his call from her gate and gave him a wave as he drove away. Wherever this relationship was headed, she was definitely ready for more of it. That thought made her heart flip a little. Just like it did whenever he was near.

She gulped. Wow, she had it bad. Who would have

thought after all her denials that she and Ethan could find a way back together?

He was a wonderful uncle, brother, and sheriff. She touched her fingers to her lips as she went inside. He was pretty wonderful at most things.

Chapter Six

As it happened, Ethan had been called upon for babysitting duties since his sister, Layla, had gotten stuck at work with an emergency. And since Maddie had paperwork to get on top of, they hadn't managed to meet up again that evening.

Looking forward to their first date she was disappointed that it didn't eventuate, but knowing that it *would* filled her with anticipation. It also stopped her dwelling too much on what was happening around town.

Friday night she went to bed early and slept in later than usual. She was doing a bit of housework upstairs in her apartment, where she spent very little time, when she heard Luke and the boys arrive.

Big Red, who had taken umbrage at the vacuum cleaner, leaped off his sulking position on the back of the couch and padded downstairs to see what the fuss was about.

Today was the first session for the twins to bake and sell their cookies and Layla spent time after dropping them off giving a verbal list of instructions to them regarding safety and respect. Once she'd gone it sounded like it was working. For several minutes.

The excited young voices got louder and louder. Luke's deeper, patient one, followed theirs and although whatever he said made a slight difference, it did make Maddie wonder, not for the first time, what she'd let herself in for. Hopefully, the bakery could withstand hurricane 'Jesse-James.'

Luke was at the oven checking the temperature when Maddie came downstairs. Big Red sat on the bottom step looking peeved by the sight before him. She scratched between his ears, but he turned away. Sometimes he was worse than a child.

Squeezing past him she went across the room to where the twins were elbow deep in flour, mixing the batter in their bowls. She stood between the boys, inwardly grimacing at the flour snow on the counter, which was a little high for them.

"What kind of cookies are you making?"

She and Luke had planned for each variation, but it was difficult to tell right then.

They swung around to grin at her, spraying cookie dough from their fingers.

"I'm making chocolate chip and Jesse's making sugar cookies."

It was good to know that Jesse wore a blue t-shirt while James had on a green one. For another day she'd be able to tell them apart, but there had to be a better way.

"I wanted to make peanut butter cookies, but Luke said I should think of the people eating them. Can't old people eat peanut butter at all?"

Maddie snorted. "Let's not call them old when we get to

the community center. And I'm sure most can eat it. Some might not like the flavor, though."

"And Luke said it might stick to their false teeth?"

It was difficult not to laugh at the vision that gave her.

"Maybe. Anyway, I think the flavors you've chosen will be perfect for them, which is more important."

The boys grinned.

"We're gonna make loads of money," Jesse stated gleefully.

Maddie nodded, not wishing to dampen their enthusiasm. "Hopefully, but first you must bake the best cookie ever."

"They're doing pretty well already." Luke showed her their first attempt that he'd just pulled from the oven.

The batch wasn't too bad at all. They weren't as round as hers or precisely uniform in size, but she'd seen a lot worse. Luke was doing a fine job as their teacher, and she was proud of all three of them.

The boys stood in front of the tray, bouncing from one leg to another.

"Can we try them? Otherwise we won't know if they're good enough," Jesse pleaded.

Maddie picked up a couple of napkins and handed them one each. "Absolutely. A baker always tastes his or her food."

The twins gave each other a high five, smacking flour across their faces and clothes as they took the warm cookies and stuffed them into their mouths.

She frowned, taking a step back. "Perhaps you could mix at the table which is a bit lower? And next time you should both wear aprons."

Luke was wearing one of the bakery aprons Maddie had purchased for them all with the Maple Lane Bakery logo emblazoned in pink across it. There happened to be a whole shelf of them in the alcove. She liked to have a clean one every day as well as spares in case they had an accident, which often happened with frosting or mixing.

She also wanted all her staff to look clean when serving in the shop, so Gran took the dirty ones home and brought them back in pristine condition, something Maddie was grateful for.

"Oops. That's my fault. I should have thought about the aprons. I hope Mrs. Dixon won't be mad?" Luke was shamefaced.

Maddie laughed and, using a cloth, wiped small faces attached to resistant bodies, but she wouldn't be deterred. At least now they could see what they were doing. A little flour still clung to lashes and hair which they didn't give a hoot about, or the crumbs that dropped from their cookies and tumbled down their t-shirts. She tried to ignore the fact that some, (quite a bit), made it to the floor along with flour and cookie dough.

"Will there be many people at the community center today?" Jesse asked around his mouthful.

"The group has more than thirty members, I believe. Since it's not their usual day for afternoon tea, I don't think we can expect all of them to turn up today. Still ... they can tell their friends for next week. And since we put up a few flyers and Angel and Isaac have them up in their stores, there might be other people dropping by."

"Are your bowls ready for the next batch?" Luke called them back to the counter.

"I sure hope tons of people buy them." James's tongue poked out and caught between his teeth as he mixed dry ingredients and added the eggs that Luke had cracked from a separate dish beside him. They were ridiculously cute, and she hoped they would have success. Luke had everything under control, so she left them to it.

She had begun to devise a plan for the new cooking class for ten paying attendees. It would mean sacrificing the Girlz' Saturday night group, but one class a week was more than enough when she put in such long days. Plus, she wanted to make time for Ethan. If they were to take their relationship any further, she had to do her share.

With so many enquiries about the class, she was excited by the prospect and not worried about getting the numbers. Passing it by the Girlz might be a little trickier, since they had loved their private lessons.

Ethan arrived as she was putting fancy plates on the back seat of Honey. He gave her a quick kiss.

"I hear you've branched out into the cookie-selling business on Saturdays now?" he teased.

"Not me exactly. But there are two new bakers using my premises, and they'll be cooking up a storm for the next couple of months."

"Be careful. A storm might be a very appropriate analogy if I know my nephews."

Maddie laughed. "They'll be under Luke's tutelage, so I feel like they're in good hands."

"I have no doubt, but you should be prepared for the worst, then you might be pleasantly surprised."

"It's not like you to be so pessimistic."

He grimaced. "Oh, it's not pessimism. When it comes to my nephews, I feel a compunction to speak the truth. It seems only fair to share my knowledge with the uninitiated, especially when your kitchen is usually so pristine, the polar opposite of any space they inhabit."

He winked at her and, despite the small lurch in her stomach, she laughed again.

"Your warning is duly noted."

Angel and Laura waved from across the road where the yoga class Noah Jackson taught had just finished. Maddie had worked hard in her apartment this morning, yet she couldn't help feeling lazy around her friends. They came over to the low stone wall which separated her property from the street. Both women gave a grin, and Angel nudged Laura. Maddie figured that it was all about Ethan being there and decided to ignore them.

"Lovely day," Angel said. She always wore a sunny smile, which today, more than any other, perfectly matched her yellow top and multicolored leggings.

"You should put your jacket on," Laura said to Angel as she shrugged into her own. "You don't want to get a chill."

Laura was a good friend, if a little anxious about too many things. Her clothing was more somber—black leggings and a black top. But with her red hair adding a riot of color, she was just as attractive ... especially when she smiled.

Helping Laura become more confident and smile more often was a mission Maddie had every confidence would succeed. After all, Laura lived with Gran and was Angel's friend, so how could it not?

Not one for being told what to do, even if it was with good intentions, Angel wrapped her jacket around a trim waist. "I'll be fine. I'm still too warm. How's the kitchen surviving, Maddie?"

"Oh, yes, it's cookie day with the twins." Laura looked towards the window.

Maddie pretended horror. "Don't remind me. I saw the kitchen earlier and let's just say that the place isn't how I left it last night."

Ethan raised his hands. "I tried to warn you."

"You should have tried harder." She grinned at him.

Just then, Beth Roberts, Angel's intern from the salon, came around the corner. She stopped midstep, her eyes widening like a deer caught in headlights. Beth had hardly been seen outside of work since she went to court several weeks back. Having to explain her involvement in the petnapping had taken its toll, and she was naturally wary about being around people and having them judge her.

"Morning, Beth. I thought you were taking the day off. Did you want me for something?" Angel asked.

"No. I ..." The girl snapped out of her shock but was clearly uncomfortable.

"Everything okay?" Ethan pressed.

Beth looked down at her feet. "Yes."

"Have you come to see Luke?" Maddie took a wild guess. The girl was here for a reason and, if it wasn't to see Angel, that narrowed it down considerably.

She looked up, warily, giving Maddie the impression that she'd like to run away. Then Beth squared her shoulders.

"Yes. He said he was having a baking lesson with the twins, and I thought I could join in. Maybe help. If that's okay with you?"

"Divide and conquer type of thing?" Ethan teased.

She frowned. "Pardon?"

"Never mind the sheriff's sense of humor." Maddie waved her up the path. "Go ahead. I'm sure Luke could use all the help he can get."

Beth gave her a grateful look as she skirted them all and went inside.

"I guess it's going to take some time before she gets over the embarrassment of being involved with Luke's brother in the pet stealing," Angel noted.

"It's only been a few weeks." Ethan reminded them.

"Nobody blames her, do they? Or Luke, for that matter?" Angel didn't appreciate animosity.

Ethan frowned. "There will always be the few who aren't accepting of someone who has associated with a felon."

"I imagine Luke is the one hardest hit by the reaction of those kind of people."

Laura was Luke's biggest champion which may have been due to her own trouble with fitting in.

Maddie sighed. "He is affected, but he's put a brave face on things and tried to be loyal to all parties. Now everyone knows about his brother, I guess as much as it is an embarrassment, it's also a relief."

Angel shivered, despite the sun, and slipped on her jacket, to Laura's approval.

"I hope things have settled down in our little town for a while."

"Me too," Laura agreed.

Maddie and Ethan looked at each other. It was a split second—nothing more.

"What was that about?" Angel demanded.

"Sorry?" Maddie could feel her cheeks warm.

"That look I just saw. Don't play innocent with me, my friend."

Ethan coughed. "You haven't seen anything odd around town, have you?"

"I knew it! Like what?" Angel was instantly intrigued.

"Like a van ... parked for a long time in one place?"

She tapped a long pink nail on her bottom lip. "A white one?"

Ethan took a long stride towards her, but the wall hampered him getting any closer. "Let me get this straight. You have seen a white van?"

Maddie slapped a hand to her forehead. "Wait a minute. Mavis was saying that a white van has been parked at the retirement community for a whole day."

He spun back towards her. "You just remembered that?"

Maddie nodded, as surprised as Ethan at having forgotten it. "And I think it might be Owen Kirk's."

"Should I know that name?"

"He's the regular delivery man from my main supplier. He even has a scar over his right eyebrow." She grimaced at her inability to put the two together until now.

"Okay, you two. Now you have to tell us what exactly is going on?" Angel demanded.

Laura had lost the thread of the conversation, but she swung her legs over the wall, eager to get as close as she could and hear more. Angel quickly followed.

He beckoned them closer, and the Girlz formed a semi-circle around him.

"First, at this moment there is no crime, and we're not looking for one." He glanced at Maddie then refocused on Laura and Angel. "We've become aware of some unusual activity, and I'm looking into it."

"You and Maddie found it?" Laura asked.

Angel tutted impatiently. "That's the 'we' he's talking about."

Ethan had a pained expression. "That's true, but from here on, I'll be the one dealing with it."

"You haven't told us what 'it' is," Laura pressed.

He wasn't in uniform, but Maddie wasn't surprised to see him take off his cap and give it a few hard twists. At least it saved his sheriff's hat, which was usually the recipient of this harsh treatment when he was vexed.

"There isn't much to tell. At this stage it looks like we

have a delivery man hanging around a couple of shops and driving over grassy areas where he shouldn't."

"That's it?"

He looked affronted. "Angel, all investigations aren't necessarily filled with excitement. Often there's a simple explanation for odd things that happen."

"Then why the secrecy?"

"Because, if the person of interest knows he's being watched or that people are aware of his activities, then they may get more cunning and deceptive," Maddie explained.

Ethan nodded. "Exactly. This is not an official investigation, but we can still take precautions for those very reasons."

Angel hardly had time to digest that before she offered, "Do you want our help?"

Ethan gave her a wary look. "In what way?"

"We could ask our customers if they've seen a white van. Maybe someone knows the driver and it's not Owen after all."

Maddie smiled. "That's an excellent suggestion."

"He doesn't strike me as a criminal," Laura interjected. "The orders are always correct."

"Criminals come in all kinds of packages. Which doesn't mean we should be suspicious of everyone," Ethan hastened to add.

Angel gave him a measured look then shrugged. "Alright. If there's no actual crime, I'm heading home for a shower before my first client arrives."

"Me too. I promised Gran I'd help her and Maddie at the community center this afternoon." Laura followed her out of the garage.

"What was that about?" Ethan asked.

"How do you mean?"

His hat suffered another twisting session. "Their capitulation. It was a little quick, especially for Angel."

Maddie laughed. "You probably don't need to worry, but they are going to bug me."

"About the investigation?"

"Possibly, but I think it'll be more about you and me."

His eyes twinkled. "Ahhh. Well, you heard Cora yesterday. What are we waiting for?"

He took a step to close the gap between them and took her face in his hands. Their eyes locked for several moments, then her eyelids fluttered as his lips dipped down to touch hers.

It was a wonderful kiss. Not a peck, as all the others had been. Not the kiss of the teenagers they were so many years ago. This was the kiss of a man and a woman who were at the beginning of something. It felt so right that she leaned against him, not wanting it to end.

When he released her, she was disappointed for a moment ... until he rubbed a thumb over her bottom lip, sending a shiver all the way to her toes.

"Let's go somewhere. Tonight. Just us."

As much as it sounded like the best idea ever, she had other plans.

"I've got the baking class. What about tomorrow night."

He frowned. "Sunday?"

"What's wrong with Sunday?"

"Nothing. It just seems so far away."

He couldn't have said anything sweeter, and she loved that he wasn't afraid to tell her he was just as eager to be with her as she was to be with him.

"I'm not doing anything now. We could have brunch at the diner?"

His head tilted. "We could."

"I hear a 'but' in there. Ethan, if you have other plans, that's fine."

"Nothing concrete, but I was thinking of heading over to the Sunny Days Retirement Community."

"Is that all? I could come for the drive, then we could have brunch after?"

"Don't you have to go to the community center?"

She shook her head. "I'm not expected until this afternoon and not urgently if Laura's going to be there too."

"Still, it's not quite what I pictured as a first date."

She smiled and took his hand. "Me either, but I don't mind."

"Strangely enough, neither do I." He kissed her knuckles. "I'll wait for you in the car. Seeing me might work the boys up into a frenzy."

"Good point."

She ran inside to tell the bakers, trying not to notice the mess. But she did note with interest that Beth and Luke looked very comfortable with each other.

"Luke, would you mind driving Honey to take the cookies over to the center when they're done? Or you could take them in your car if you prefer?"

"Are you serious? I'd love to drive Honey. She's a classic." His face reddened at his obvious enthusiasm. "Aren't you coming to the center?"

She was delighted that Luke thought Honey so awesome. The jeep was incredibly special to Maddie. She did not hand out her keys lightly or very often.

"I'm going out for a few hours, but I'll meet you at the center for afternoon tea if you think everything will be okay here?"

She had promised Layla she would be around, but with

Beth here they had a one on one experience that should be safe enough.

"We've got the last batches in the oven now. We'll package them up, then I thought I'd make sandwiches for lunch. I baked a loaf of bread already." Luke cast a sidelong glance at Beth.

"Well done. That sounds like a great idea. Help yourself to anything out of the walk-in. And Beth, please stay as long as you like."

Beth smiled and Luke looked pleased. The twins were crouched in front of the oven, the aprons Luke had put on them after her suggestion earlier flowed around them and were filthy. The happiness on their faces made the dirty aprons not such an issue. Although, she hadn't run that by Gran at any stage.

With everything organized, she ran out to Ethan's dark-blue sedan.

Chapter Seven

The van was parked exactly where Mavis had said. Ethan pulled into a visitors' space, and they went over to it. The windows were fogged up, which was odd since it wasn't particularly cold. The engine was running.

Maddie and Ethan walked around the vehicle to the driver's side. A shadow was slumped against the wheel. Ethan opened the door to reveal Owen Kirk, who didn't move.

"Stand back," he yelled as he held on to Owen with one hand, to prevent him from sliding out the door, and turned off the ignition with the other.

Maddie backed away as Ethan lowered Owen to the ground. He felt for a pulse then glanced up, shaking his head.

Maddie's heart raced. She knew the answer but still had to ask while calling for the paramedics. "He's dead?"

Ethan nodded. "Has been for a while I think."

She turned away, not wanting to see Owen like this. He

had always been an amiable, reliable man. Although she'd only known him for a few months, she had seen him every week.

With the call made, she snuck a look at Ethan who was crouching beside Owens' feet. He took a small tool from his pocket and placed a sample of something off the shoes into a plastic bag he'd wrestled from another pocket.

"What's that?"

He sealed the bag. "Remember at the gallery how I said that the person there would have tobacco on their boot?"

"Owen? He does smoke, but I wouldn't know the brand."

Ethan held up the bag before placing it in his pocket. "This will tell us." He put gloves on and went to check the front inside of the vehicle.

Maddie followed. There were cigarettes and a packet of matches on the dashboard.

"I guess that confirms that Owen is our loitering man?"

"Not at all. We can't be sure that the ash at the gallery matches these cigarettes. Or that Owen smoked there."

He was perhaps saying this for his own benefit, but she was completely baffled, and her hands were tapping on her leg.

"Did he have a heart attack?"

"I don't think so. Suicide by carbon monoxide poisoning? Maybe. There's no hose inside the vehicle, so perhaps not. It's too early to say, but there're definitely fumes involved somehow."

She was beside him as he pointed at Owen. "How can you tell?"

"His cheeks are pink."

"Okay?"

Ethan went to the back doors and pulled them open, fanning them to dissipate the fumes more quickly. "When someone has a heart attack, they turn a little blue around the mouth and their cheeks are pale. With gas, a protein called myoglobin causes the skin to look pink creating a false image of good circulation rather than one starved of oxygen, like a heart attack victim. Stand back. The gas must be stronger here because my head is already aching."

She moved away a little and pulled the neck of her blouse over her nose and mouth. "So, it was accidental?" she asked through the fabric.

"Maybe."

"But it could have been something else?"

"Yes."

Maddie was used to his monosyllabic replies when he was working on a case. She found it frustrating and interesting in equal measure. To figure out what he was thinking and imagine what had happened was intriguing. Her curiosity and deductive reasoning were definitely something she had inherited from her ex-Secret Service grandfather.

In her mind, judging by the evidence so far, and what Ethan said, it was likely carbon monoxide that killed him. Yet, Owen had never appeared to be someone who suffered from depression. Then again, people could hide their feelings from even their loved ones, and she and Owen had not been that close.

On the other hand, if Owen hadn't killed himself, how had he died? As well as teaching her to drive, her grandfather had passed on a working knowledge of cars so that the likelihood of her being stranded on country lanes without a good chance of getting home was minimalized.

She knew it would take a lot of gas to kill a person quickly so that they didn't have time to escape. A slow leak wouldn't do it in a vehicle.

Her grandfather also taught her to trust her instincts. If it wasn't an accident, and she didn't see how it could have been, then someone must have had a hand in his death.

Gran would not be impressed with some of the other things he had taught her. Things that had helped her get out of sticky situations and might help here.

While Ethan called for back-up, Maddie went to Ethan's car and grabbed tissues from her bag then found a large stick under a nearby maple tree. She came back and handed him a wad of tissues, keeping the rest for herself.

"Do you have any spare gloves?" she asked when he'd finished.

He raised an eyebrow, shook his head once more, and handed her another pair from his pocket. She slipped them on and with the stick grasped firmly in her hand she climbed onto the rear bumper of the van. Using the stick, she hooked the rubber mat which covered most of the empty floor. It folded back surprisingly easily, given its weight, to reveal a large hole in the floor.

"That hole was cut recently."

Ethan leaned over her shoulder. "How can you tell?"

"Look at the edges. They're shiny. Unprotected, metal will always get grimy and eventually rust."

He squeezed her shoulder. "Great pick up. Anything else?"

"There was something in here recently. Something rectangular, heavy, and in cardboard."

He leaned in further. Their shoulders brushed against each other. In the confines of the rear of the van, his musky cologne was welcome, and yet very distracting.

Ethan pointed along the mat. "I can see the dents, and the fragments of boxes or, as you so rightly said, cardboard. And they were tied to the brackets at the sides, judging by these remnants of string."

Sirens sounded nearby and they climbed down in mutual agreement. A few minutes was long enough to spend in the lingering fumes which had made her head pound.

The paramedics were followed by Deputy Jacobs, who pulled up outside the gates to allow the ambulance to get through. Soon Ethan was relaying all the information in more detail. She noticed he kept their conjecture to himself.

The sirens had also made it known to the whole Sunny Days retirement community that they were on site, and there had been an incident. The gathering of onlookers, getting bigger by the minute, wasn't shy about asking questions. Since Ethan was unavailable, apparently, Maddie was the next best thing.

Mavis was first. "Is he dead?"

The sheet over his face might have made this obvious, but Maddie didn't point that out.

"Unfortunately, yes he is."

"The poor man. He was having trouble with his van, maybe that's what gave him the heart attack?"

It was as much a statement to her co-villagers as it was a question to Maddie.

"The sheriff isn't sure how he died, so it's better that we don't guess at this stage."

The woman nodded emphatically. "Of course not. Owen. That's his name, isn't it, Maddie?"

"Yes."

"You know him well, don't you, dear?" Mavis pressed.

"Not well, but I've met him a few times."

This was all information anyone could easily find out, so Maddie didn't feel like she was stepping on toes, though she didn't want to be seen as a spokesperson for the police. Mavis wasn't done, and everyone else seemed content to let her have the floor.

"He was your delivery man."

Maddie found it hard not to snap at the sweet, if persistent, woman. "He was *a* delivery man."

"Seems like you've known all the people who've died recently," Nora intoned in that deathbed way she had.

"It's a small town. Most of us know the people who die here." Mavis nodded at her own wisdom.

Nora shook her head. "I don't know this man at all, and neither did you until you spoke to him yesterday."

"Well, he seemed nice, and he spoke highly of Maddie's bakery."

"I hope the cookies on sale at the center today will be of a similar quality," Nora droned.

"Are you both going this afternoon?" Maddie asked, encouraging the change of subject.

Mavis nodded eagerly. "Yes, we are. Sunny Days is supplying the coach to take us there and back. Bernie's driving."

"He'd better not speed this time."

Mavis rolled her eyes at Nora. "Bernie never goes over the limit."

"Then the limit's too high. I'd like to arrive in one piece."

Maddie let their voices wash over her as she watched Ethan work. It was creating a distraction for the other residents who had come by to watch, and at least this conversation didn't seem to require her input.

Eventually, when Ethan and Rob had staked out an area

around the van and taken pictures, the ambulance was allowed to take Owen away. Then Ethan came over to Maddie and the residents.

"I'd appreciate it, folks, if you stayed away from this area and let the deputies work. We'll let you know what happened when we have all the details," he assured them. "Right now, there's nothing more to add, so you can get back to what you were doing, please."

Slowly they dispersed, with Nora muttering her doom and gloom and Mavis chattering away like a small bird.

Ethan smiled wryly. "Thanks for keeping them occupied. I'm sorry Maddie, but I'll have to renege on lunch." Ethan's focus was already shifting back to the van and Owen's mysterious death.

"That's okay. We can catch up tomorrow night like we'd planned."

He nodded. "Definitely. I better get back. The detective will be here soon."

"Detective Jones?"

"You remember him?"

"He's hard to forget, even if he doesn't talk much."

Steve Jones was a somber man, as tall as Ethan and rather good looking. He had a quiet way of studying people and his surroundings that could be a little unnerving. He also didn't seem inclined to get too close to the people of Maple Falls.

"That's true, but he's the best detective assigned to the county that I've ever worked with," Ethan assured her.

"Then he must be good." She gave a small smile. "Well if we aren't doing lunch, I need to get to the community center. It's nearly time for the afternoon tea that I promised to help with."

"I understand, and there's nothing for you to do here. I

need to stay and wait for Jones, but Jacobs can drop you off on his way to the station. Thanks for being here with me and for your insights."

They stood looking awkwardly at each other for a moment, and she wondered if he was thinking about that kiss. Despite Owen's death, she certainly was. She hoped that didn't make her a bad person.

A cough from behind startled them. Deputy Rob Jacobs stood there, unsuccessfully trying to hide a grin. Ethan gave him a warning look then explained about Maddie needing a ride.

"Sure. There are plenty of deputies to help now and my car's outside the gate."

"Thanks, Rob." She gave Ethan a small wave as she walked with Rob to his car. "I could have caught a ride with Bernie, but if you're going my way ...?

He opened the car door for her. "I'm working on another aspect of the case, so I have to get back to the station. Is this a special afternoon tea, or something you do every week? I was under the impression Tuesday was the day for the get together?"

She laughed. "You're well informed. Gran runs it on Tuesdays and has done so for years. I like to help when I can, depending on any catering bookings I have. But this is a new thing starting today."

Maddie told him about the twins and their money-making enterprise.

"I know what a fantastic cook Gran is, but I bet they love your baking at the center just as much. I know I do. And as far as the boys are concerned, I'm glad it's your place and not mine they're using to bake in. I hope you're heavily insured." He laughed at his joke then gave her a horrified glance. "Don't tell the sheriff I said that."

Maddie smiled, but wasn't quite so amused. She had faith in Luke. And yet her fingers involuntarily crossed in the hopes that the bakery would be no worse for wear by the time she got back to it.

Chapter Eight

They arrived at the community center with a little time to spare. Maddie had sampled the cookies and they tasted good. Not to Maddie's standard for selling in the bakery, but she suspected Luke had done more than oversee them to ensure they had come out as well as they had.

Rob hung around for a little while, even helping put out the tables and chairs. He had looked around the kitchen, greeted Luke, the boys and Beth, but kept a watch on the door.

Maddie had a feeling he was hoping a certain redhead would stop by. Eventually, he left to get back to the office, looking disappointed.

She was looking through the window when Bernie pulled the Sunny Days transit van into the parking lot. He waved to her as he opened the doors for Mavis and her friends. Maddie waved back and ran outside to catch Mavis before she came inside.

"That's a lovely blouse, Mavis. Can I have a private word with you."

"Thank you, dear." She preened. "It's one of my favorites."

"I was wondering if you could do me a favor and not talk about what happened this morning? At least while Jesse and James are around."

"Why, of course. We don't want to upset them, do we?"

Maddie breathed a sigh of relief, grateful that she'd managed to avert what would have been a morbid topic for the twins and not appropriate right now.

It was a little difficult to concentrate with thoughts of poor Owen and what might have happened, or rather how it had happened. It was no accident. They might not have ruled out suicide, but an hour later it still seemed unlikely. She wished she knew more about Owen and why someone might want to harm him.

"Are you okay?"

Gran was making tea and coffee and frowned as soon as Maddie came back into the kitchen. It was hard to hide anything from her grandmother, but she didn't want to drag everyone down with sadness.

"I'll tell you later." She motioned to the boys and Gran nodded her understanding.

Maddie helped her with the drinks, while Beth put the cookies on plates and Luke, with the help of the boys, created a pile of the boxes on a separate table.

The cookies were a hit. Luke was extolling Beth's help in the clean-up at the bakery and Maddie was impressed that she'd made the plates look so good using some of Maddie's edible flowers to decorate them. It was a nice, thoughtful touch.

Beth stayed in the kitchen, making fresh tea, while Luke and the twins worked the room. Maddie had made sure they had a small float of coins to begin and soon the container she'd put them in was overflowing with dollar bills and more coins.

She had also donated some takeaway boxes for any that didn't get eaten, which proved unnecessary, since by the time they had finished there wasn't one cookie left apart from the pre-packaged boxes.

Layla walked in just as they were cleaning up the kitchen, and Gran was stacking plates away.

"How did it go?"

The boys jumped up and down around her.

"So cool! We made change and we were polite."

Jesse hugged Layla while James shook the container of money in her face.

"We sold every single one, mom."

"Well done. You must have had one great teacher." She smiled at Luke as the boys moved to the corner of the kitchen to count their money.

"Thanks, but they listened and worked really hard, and Beth helped."

Beth, who'd had the spirit knocked out of her by her ex, who was languishing in jail, stood shyly by the sink, shoulders hunched as if waiting for something negative to be said.

Layla went over to her and gave her a gentle hug, which caught Beth off guard.

"Thank you for helping these rascals. I should really pay you and Luke for babysitting, never mind the baking. With their uncle tied up at work, I don't know what I would have done today. It worked out well."

Beth gave a nervous laugh. "Oh, I don't mind at all. In fact, I love kids."

"Really? Layla raised her eyebrows. "Even mine?"

"Especially yours. They're so funny," Beth said, with an

enthusiasm which hadn't been evident since her troubles had become known.

"They really are," Luke agreed.

"Hmm. Let's see if they're still funny when they've been with you a few times."

"That's okay with me. If you need time out or you have a date, Beth and I could babysit?"

Layla laughed at his suggestion but had a flush to her cheeks Maddie hadn't seen before. Was there someone she was interested in?

"I'll keep that in mind, should the need arise. Come on boys, let's get you home and cleaned up. I'd better look after that." She took the only remaining container from James, tucking it under her arm as she ushered the protesting pair out the door. "Thanks everyone."

Gran smiled at Beth, Luke, and Maddie. "Well, wasn't that nice. It feels like everyone's a winner today."

Maddie thought of Owen, who's day had not turned out so well. She could see Mavis and Nora holding court at the far end of the room.

"I know that look. Don't try to distract me again. Mavis has been very cagey, but she looks set to burst, so you may as well tell me what's happened?"

Maddie made a mental note to work on her poker face. It seemed everyone could tell when she had news. She just hoped she did a better job than Mavis—who kept glancing her way, as did the other residents from Sunny Days.

"There's been a death," she said quietly, but not quietly enough.

Beth gasped. "Another murder?"

"Let's not get ahead of ourselves. Right now, there's no evidence to say it was anything sinister." As she spoke, she had the thought that she was beginning to sound like Ethan.

"Who was it?" asked Luke

Maddie sighed. It still seemed surreal, even though she had seen him for herself. "Owen Kirk."

Gran put a hand to her chest. "The delivery man?"

"Yes, I'm sorry to say."

"That is a shame. He seemed a very nice man in the short time I've known him."

"I thought so too, Gran. I couldn't say anything before with the boys here, and I didn't want to upset anyone."

She needn't have bothered with her concern. Nothing could stop the community center gossip mill once it was set in motion. When they left the kitchen the discussion over Owen's death was rampant and loud with everyone wanting to voice an opinion.

Mavis jumped up from her seat, managing to catch the plate perched on her lap, but shooting crumbs from it all over the floor.

"Here's Maddie, she was right there when the sheriff found poor Owen. Any news, dear?"

"Nothing more. I'm sorry."

She could hear a stiffness to her voice and Mavis picked up on it, looking worried.

"We didn't talk about it in front of the children, but they're gone now, aren't they?"

"Thanks, Mavis. Yes, they're gone."

"So, it's okay to discuss now?"

Maddie nodded, unsure why Mavis needed her approval and knowing that there was no point in trying to stop the flow of a lava cake, once the spoon had dipped into its enticing center. Besides, quite a few of this group lived at Sunny Days, so they would have seen the commotion with emergency services for themselves. It was a miracle that they'd managed to hold off until now.

Mavis smiled. "Is Ethan stopping by here?"

"He said he might, but he's terribly busy right now, as you can imagine."

"To question us?" Mavis asked with barely concealed glee, ignoring the fact that it wasn't a given Ethan would show at all.

"He'll no doubt have a chat with everyone from Sunny Days at some stage."

"I guess he'll have to make an arrest if it's murder." Nora sighed.

Gran tutted. "Maddie already said that they don't know the cause, so we'll just have to wait and see. Now, is everyone done here? I'd like to finish putting away the tea things."

"We should wait for the sheriff," Mavis said with uncharacteristic firmness.

Gran could also be firm. "There is no way to say how long that would be and the sheriff knows each and every one of you and where you live. I think he'll find you just fine, should he need to. And Bernie has been waiting outside for ten minutes."

With more than a few mutterings they filed out, except for Jed who was on the community center committee along with Gran. He gave the floor a quick sweep while Luke, Beth, and Maddie loaded Honey with the plates. Then they checked the facility once more.

"You know, Owen hung around town quite often," Jed offered as he put the broom away.

So, other people had noticed Owens' tendency for that. "You mean when he wasn't delivering?"

"That's it. He loved to look around the shops. I asked him one day if he had family in town."

"Did he?"

Jed frowned. "He said no, but something about the way he said it made me think it wasn't true. He also said he loved it here. Said we were a real community and wished it would always be so. I told him that Maple Falls had been this way for generations, and we weren't fixing to change that any time soon."

"Thank you, Mr. Clayton. I'll ask Ethan to come by your place so you can share your insights with him, if that's okay?"

"Sure thing. I love visitors, and Ethan has some great stories of his own to tell. He also makes a fuss of my Sissy, and she hasn't forgotten that he saved her life after she'd been stolen. With your help," he added quickly."

Maddie smiled, trying to picture Ethan regaling Jed with stories. It seemed unlikely, but she was learning that the sheriff had qualities she had never guessed at. Jed left in his '57 Chevy while the rest of them piled into Honey.

Luke handed her the keys. "I loved driving your jeep. She never missed a beat."

"My grandfather said if you look after a car, she'll last forever." Maddie started the engine, satisfied with the gentle rumble.

Gran patted her arm affectionately. "He was a wise old fool."

A lump caught in Maddie's throat. "He was wise, but no fool, Gran. He married you, didn't he?"

They smiled at each other, enjoying the shared moment of memories that happened often between them.

Oblivious to the feelings in the front of Honey, Luke caressed the worn but intact leather seats. "Who keeps her in this condition?"

"Me."

She glanced at him in the rearview mirror and caught

his look of admiration. "My Grandfather taught me about cars."

"Among other things," Gran added. "Not all of them things a young lady should have been learning."

In that moment as she felt her Gran's stare, Maddie realized that Gran never missed a thing. All this time she would have known what Maddie and her grandfather were up to when they spent hours out in the fields or in his huge workshop.

Maddie snorted. "Me? A lady? You know that was never an option."

"True." She sighed. "When you weren't climbing trees, shooting game or playing detective, you were baking. There's nothing clean and tidy about any of those things."

Beth laughed for the first time. A proper one, which was a lovely sound. And the others joined her. The rest of the drive went in a similar manner, with Luke asking her about her questionable talents and Gran making snide remarks. There was truth in what she said, but no malice.

She let Beth and Luke out by the bakery and watched as the two of them walked across the road to his car.

Gran turned a little to face Maddie, her matchmaking on high alert. "They make a cute couple. I'm so glad they didn't end up in jail."

"I believe it was touch and go with Beth." Maddie grinned mischievously. "They are cute together. I wonder if Luke had a thing for Beth even when she was seeing his brother?"

"I've wondered about them too, but right now I want all the details about Owen. I've been waiting all afternoon like a ball of dough going dry. What really happened?"

Maddie didn't know much more than what had been said at the center, but she retold Gran about the van and

Owen's penchant for loitering around town. Although, to be fair, no one had mentioned it in a sinister way. Rather, like Jed said, he was enjoying being part of the general feeling of the town.

She could appreciate that. Leaving for several years, then returning, had opened her eyes to what a great place it was. Maybe Owen lived or had grown up in a big city, where people weren't so friendly as they were here.

"It seems that you have yourself another mystery. You and the Girlz."

"Oh, it's not our mystery ..."

Gran made a rude sound. "I bet the four of you are already involved, aren't you?"

Maddie couldn't lie. "We might be checking into a few things."

Gran shook her head. "I know you like to help out. But if Owen's death isn't what we'd all like to believe—a simple case of accidental death by gas poisoning—then promise me you'll be careful?"

"Of course I will."

They had pulled up outside Gran's cottage, and Maddie walked her to the door.

"Something you want to discuss?"

She nodded. "A comment that Nora made gave me chills."

"Nora? Sweetheart, no one listens to Nora. She'd have us all jumping off cliffs like those lemmings that follow each other to their deaths, if she had her way."

"That's a fabricated story, and well you know it."

Gran snorted. "It doesn't stop you from knowing what I mean. But, since it's got you worried, what did she say?"

Maddie wrinkled her nose. "That I always know the victim."

"Sweetheart, it's a small town. It would be surprising if you didn't. Maybe everyone doesn't know Owen, but they did know the others. And they do know that you helped in both instances."

Gran could always make Maddie feel better, and wasn't that exactly what Mavis had said to Nora?

Chapter Nine

The cooking class went on as usual that night and the Girlz were in fine form. They were making chocolate truffles and since they were chocoholics, especially Angel, the news about Owen couldn't quite dampen their enthusiasm.

Naturally it was harder for Maddie to push it from her mind, since she had seen him and they hadn't. She filled their wine glasses, determined not to ruin the evening.

"I heard that you're opening up this class to others. Is this our last private class?" Angel asked.

Maddie took a sip of her wine and looked at Laura, who went almost as red as her hair which was an obvious giveaway.

"Sorry about my big mouth. I only told these guys," Laura promised.

Maddie put a hand on her shoulder. "It's fine. Nothing's been finalized yet, and I did want to talk it over with all of you. The thing is ... my spare time is pretty limited. If I run two courses, I may never have any time to do other things."

"Like yoga?" Angel teased.

Maddie had been talking about joining the Saturday morning group that met in the park just across the road from the bakery for so long it had become a source of amusement to the Girlz, who brought it up any chance they got.

"Naturally, that was top of my list," she replied, straight-faced.

"I imagine the sleuthing would eat into those hours too?" Suzy raised an eyebrow.

"What sleuthing?" She feigned innocence.

"Hah! You went with Ethan to the retirement village to scope the van and Owen's movements, so don't you deny it."

Maddie twirled her glass. "That's not exactly how it was."

"Whatever the intention, my friend," Suzy pointed at her. "You were doing some detective work out there."

She wasn't about to tell them, and have to endure the ribbing, that it had been the precursor to a date that never eventuated. "I can't help it if I seem to be in the right place when there's a mystery."

"I'm not touching that statement with a ten-foot pole." Suzy laughed.

Angel nodded. "Be honest, sugar. You love all this brouhaha."

"I wouldn't say love, but, well ... It is fascinating." Maddie finished lamely.

"Need any help?" Suzy asked.

She frowned. "Help? With what?"

"The murder investigation."

"Nobody said anything about a murder investigation."

Suzy snorted. "Not aloud. But any fool can see one and one does not equal two here."

Angel nearly spilt her wine and just managed to keep it upright. "How's that?"

Suzy put her glass down and ticked off her fingers. "Owen's been in town on and off for several months. Each time he's here he stays most of the day. He often parked his van outside Mom's gallery. He goes in every time, browses and buys nothing."

"It's not a cheap place to shop," Laura commented.

"Maybe not, but wouldn't he know that from the very first time?"

Angel tutted. "There's no harm in looking at pretty things, surely?"

"No there isn't, and I could be way off base, but he didn't strike me as the type to like pretty things."

Angel frowned. "Suzy, I'm surprised at you. Any type of person can like the things in a Gallery. Even burly men."

Suzy nodded. "Usually, I would agree with you, but I met Owen several times when I was helping Mom at the gallery. He was clumsy and only interested in the paintings —the pricey paintings."

Maddie's skin prickled, a sure sign that she was right about Owen not being who they all thought. "I hear an 'and' coming."

"*And* he asked a lot of questions about the artists. He never wrote anything down but seemed to be taking mental notes and asked me to repeat things several times.

"Has anything gone missing from the gallery?" Laura asked.

"Not that I know of."

Maddie tapped her fingers on her thigh, which helped when she was formulating an idea. "Could you ask your mom?"

Suzy's eyes widened. "Actually, because of his many

visits, I did mention to her that it seemed odd. Mom agreed, but she liked Owen, and is quite upset about his passing. Maybe I could bring it up in a few days."

"Liked?" Angel queried. "In what way?"

"Don't be silly. Mom and Dad are as happy as ever."

Suzy sounded overly defensive about her parents, which wasn't necessary as far as Maddie was concerned. They'd been married forty years, and there had never been so much as a whiff of any scandal surrounding them. They occasionally bickered like all couples but had never raised their voices around Maddie.

Angel was contrite, if a little confused. "Oh, Sugar, I didn't mean in a bad way. No, I meant she didn't know him for long. It seems odd that she would be so upset."

"Working in a gallery in a small town can be a lonely job. Some days there are very few customers and the artists are infrequent. They come in with a few works at a time, which might be weeks, if not months, apart. Owen came in every week and they'd get to chatting. Perhaps he was lonely too."

Suzy was almost talking to herself, as if she was also looking for an explanation regarding the friendship that had clearly cropped up between Owen and Cora. An explanation that may or may not be the truth. Only Cora would know for sure.

Maddie wanted to ease the worry for her friend. "He'd want to keep a low profile if he planned to steal anything, so that couldn't have been why he was there."

Suzy gave her a small smile. "Do you have any idea why he was hanging around my mom?"

Maddie tapped her thigh. "Nothing that makes any sense. Does she have any high-profile artists on her books?"

Suzy flicked her dark bob while she thought. Then her eyes lit up. "Yes. Nicholas Brack."

Laura gasped. "Seriously? He's mega famous. Does he live in Maple Falls?"

"He moved back here a year ago. His family owns a place out by the lake. Now he's one who likes to keep a low profile." Suzy put a hand to her mouth. "Gosh, I hope it's not a secret."

Maddie shook her head. "I wouldn't think so. Most people who admire his work and live locally would have seen him around, surely?"

"I don't have a clue who he is. Then again, art has never been my strong suit," Angel acknowledged.

Laura smiled. "I love his work, but I didn't notice anything of his last time I was in."

"They go pretty fast, and Mom hasn't had one of his for ages. Apparently, he only does commissions for private customers these days."

Maddie was busy taking mental notes when she had an idea. "Are you working at the gallery anytime soon, Suzy?"

"Monday after school for a couple of hours while Mom has an appointment. Why?"

"Can we all come in and look about. It would save upsetting your mom any further."

Suzy shrugged. "I guess that would be okay, but I don't know what you think you'll find."

Angel pursed her lips. "Monday is my slow day. I'll check my appointments and see if I can work around it."

"Perfect. Are you in, Laura?" Maddie asked.

She grinned. "I'd like to come, but that would mean leaving Luke on his own for an hour or so?"

Maddie slapped a hand to her forehead. Sometimes she

forgot she had a bakery that wouldn't run itself just because she was involved in a mystery.

"I'll ask him if he'd mind holding down the fort because I think it would be good if you came. You'll probably have a better idea of a good painting than any of us."

"Including me," Suzy admitted. "Much to my mother's horror. I've worked in the gallery for years, and I still don't get some of the work which Mom claims is so wonderful."

Laura titled her head. "Art is subjective. You might like something I wouldn't and vice versa."

"Yes, but some of us have never been around much art in our lives," Maddie explained.

Suzy laughed. "As Laura implied it's not usual to love something because of a price tag."

"Well, we can chew on the lack of appreciation all night, but I think we should get back to baking." Maddie stood and handed them their aprons.

The Girlz were getting much better at following the instructions and Maddie had deliberately chosen something not too hard as well as something she had plenty of ingredients for, since her stocks were getting low.

With the recipe complete, Angel, Suzy, Laura, and Maddie sat at the counter rolling their truffles in chocolate or coconut. Angel did some in both.

These hadn't required baking, which was a nice change. Other than Honey, Maddie's oven was her pride and joy. It had a glass front and stood five feet high. It could handle many trays at a time, which was a good thing if Maddie was to open up this freebie cooking class to paying customers.

"So, when do you think our last class together will be?"

Maddie laughed at Angel hitting on exactly what was going through her mind. "Don't be dramatic. We'll still be together, but there will be a few others here too."

Her eyes widened. "You mean we can come as well?"

"Only if you want to," Maddie teased.

"Of course we do, don't we?" Suzy asked the others.

"Will it be the same do you think? I don't begrudge the newbies, but I will miss this time when it's just us." Angel's mouth quivered.

Maddie put an arm around her. "I know, but the aim is by not having another class the four of us would have time to do other things, which could be together or something on our own, that we've wanted to do for a while." She was thinking about Ethan, but Angel was fortunately focused on the four of them.

"I like the sound of that. What kinds of things?"

"How about dancing lessons?" Maddie wasn't sure if she wanted to but had to throw something into the mix since it was her suggestion.

Laura gave them a shy smile. "Swimming lessons?"

Angel frowned. "We can all swim. With the lake on our doorstep we had to learn at school."

"Yes, I did too, but the new coach at the country club is quite a hunk."

"Laura!" Angel spluttered over her wine.

She shrugged. "I'm just saying. A little eye candy while we're there wouldn't hurt."

"I thought you had your sights set on Deputy Jacobs?" Angel had a mischievous smile.

"I have no idea what you mean." Laura's cheeks began to rival her hair.

Maddie snorted, trying to keep a straight face, but when Angel and Suzy laughed, she lost the battle. Laura was so straitlaced at times that talking about a hunk in any capacity was a treat. It was a shame that this new insight into her personality had backfired and Angel was like a dog with a bone.

"When he said he was taking those puppies home after the blackmail and petnapping incident, you two were inseparable and have been giving each other puppy eyes ever since."

Laura's mouth gaped for a moment. "That's plain crazy. I was glad the puppies had a new home and would be looked after. Rob seemed to be the best solution. And naturally I like to know how they're doing."

Angel grinned. "Rob? Not Deputy Jacobs? Well, Rob is cute, fit, loves animals, and has the hots for you. What else do you need?"

Maddie imagined that Angel and Laura had had this conversation more than once since, embarrassed though Laura was, she also had a shy smile that flickered in and out as she tried to be outraged.

"If I knew that, life would be good deal easier. How about I'll let you know when I decide? Right now, I'm happy just learning to bake."

"And help Maddie solve crimes." Angel winked.

"Do we know that it *is* a crime?" Laura argued.

Maddie grimaced. "Whether a crime has been committed or not has yet to be determined, but Owen did not kill himself. That much I am sure of." She could have kicked herself for mentioning it again, but the Girlz were happy to rehash the events without being morbid.

The wine may have helped.

Chapter Ten

The resort by the lake had experienced many problems in its short life. New owners had recently finished extensive renovations, and it was now open to the public once more. It had a very nice restaurant attached, and Maddie was pleased that this date, their first official one, was taking them just far enough from Maple Falls to give at least the illusion of more privacy.

Ethan wore dress pants and a sky-blue shirt which matched his eyes. She wore the blue jersey dress he had once complimented her on, and left her long blonde hair out of the braid she normally wore to cascade down her back, .

She took his arm as he helped her from his car. "It's nice to get dressed up once in a while."

His eyes twinkled down at her. "You look lovely."

"So do you."

The corner of his mouth twitched in the way she'd always found fascinating. "I remember that you always said that back in the day."

They walked up the path and into the warmth of the dining room. A large open fireplace on one wall gave the place a friendly and inviting ambience. The waiter took them to a table overlooking the lake and left them to study the menu.

"This place is incredible. The last time I was here it smelled of damp and the service was lousy," she whispered, since there were two couples already seated nearby.

"It was pretty awful for a long time. I heard the previous owners ended up selling the place for a song because of bad plumbing and building work in general. The new owner's done an incredible job in a short space of time. News has spread how great the food is, so he's always booked well in advance."

While Ethan had been talking the place had begun to fill. She didn't recognize anyone but noticed the women wore a lot of gold on their hands, wrists, and necks.

"What's wrong? You look worried."

"I'm thinking that this place is going to be terribly expensive."

"Don't think about it at all. You and Gran are always feeding me, so I am paying tonight, and I won't argue about it." He sat back and folded his arms.

She raised an eyebrow. They had always shared costs, but this was a new relationship in a new era for them. "Just this once. I never dreamed I'd eat in a place like this. Or be sitting across the table from you."

"We had a lot of dreams back then and, even though I was mad at you for the longest time, I never thought of being with anyone else permanently."

"Ethan, I know about your girlfriends."

"Just as I know about your fiancé. It's not the same thing though, is it?"

"I guess you're right." She wasn't ready to confess her love for Ethan, but now she knew how it could be, she had to admit that she had never loved Dalton. 'Some people fit, and others don't. Some dreams come true."

He reached across and picked up her hand. "Achieving our goals and doing what we love doesn't mean it's the end of our dreams, does it?"

She laughed. "Not at all. It simply means we can move on to the next one."

"I like the sound of that." He gave her a serious look. "I really am sorry that I didn't support you in your career choice. Especially when I knew your true love was baking and not sitting behind a desk. Letting you go wasn't something I was capable of as a teenager."

"I was an idiot not to know that about myself. I had to figure myself out. I wasted a few years trying to be something I wasn't. But that's behind us. I'm glad we can forgive each other and put that resentment in the past."

Running around in her mind were reasons why this still might not be a good idea. The relationship they'd had through high school had finished abruptly when she went to work in New York City. Fighting over her decision to leave to further her career had tainted everything for a very long time. In fact, it had taken a couple of months for them to even have a conversation when she moved back home.

Since then, they had forged a friendship that was working, one she didn't want to lose. While they'd both matured and accepted the other's view of that time, he was still, in many ways, the same Ethan he'd always been, and Maddie didn't want either of them to go through that heartache again.

The waiter came with the bottle of white wine Ethan had ordered and, after pouring them a glass, took their selections.

When he'd gone, Ethan raised his glass to hers. "Since

we can't change it and we've always had feelings for each other, let's toast the beginning of a new, stronger relationship."

"I can't deny that I have feelings for you. Heck, it's obvious to everyone around us. But are you sure about this?"

He grinned. "You know I am. From the moment I walked into your bakery and saw you covered in paint I wanted you back in my life."

They clinked their glasses while Maddie's insides turned to syrup. The light, golden kind.

"That might be the sweetest thing you've ever said to me."

He shrugged. "Don't get used to it."

"That attitude won't win me over, Sheriff."

His dimple flashed. "I know what will."

"Ooh, a little mystery?" She leaned across the table.

"I'm not sure this is the right setting for my disclosure, and you'd have to keep it to yourself." Ethan twirled the liquid in his glass.

"Of course I will, now stop teasing me and spill."

He leaned as close as he could and lowered his voice. "There was no way Owen Kirk killed himself."

Maddie hadn't been expecting this revelation, but she was immediately invested in the outcome. "How do you know for sure?"

"Owen had a massive lump on the back of his head and was most likely unconscious before being placed at the steering wheel. He wouldn't have smelled the carbon monoxide—even if he had woken—because it's odorless. And the pipe that was pushed through from the exhaust was covered in oil. There was no residue on Owen. Naturally, this isn't official yet."

She nodded. This case was smelling more of foul play

every minute. "Why do you think he was in the carpark in the first place?"

He took her hand across the table and ran his thumb over it, causing a delicious tingle despite the conversation.

"That's a much tougher question. He had a box of your cookies on the front seat and a thermos of coffee. Clearly, he had been expecting to be there for some time."

Maddie put a hand to her mouth. "My cookies? Why would he have them?"

Ethan shrugged. "Did he buy some last time he dropped off a delivery?"

"Not that I know of. I haven't seen him for nearly a week, but he surely wasn't eating stale cookies?"

"I'll come by tomorrow and ask Laura and Luke if they sold him any and if so when. It might be nothing but could give us a better time frame."

The waiter arrived with their order, and they reluctantly dropped hands. Having both ordered the fish, it was beginning to look like they had a lot more in common than attraction and solving mysteries.

Romance between them might be along the lines of pulling taffy—a long drawn out process—but she was finding both the romance and the mysteries fascinating. It was a little disconcerting how her mind could switch from one to the other so easily. She wondered if this was how it was for Ethan.

Less than three months ago, Maddie had been fighting these feelings for him but, turns out, the sheriff was mighty persuasive.

"There's something else," Ethan said when the waiter had topped up their glasses and left.

"The van parked between the shops?"

"Nothing gets past you, does it?" he teased.

"I wouldn't say that, but it's been playing on my mind. The Girlz and I are going to the gallery tomorrow to have a look around."

He frowned. "You were going to tell me, weren't you?"

"Yes, Sheriff. I'm doing so right now," she said, innocently.

He raised an eyebrow. "Hmmm. The tire tracks across the park were from Owen's van at the gallery."

"But not at the Country Club?"

"Exactly. Owen has never been seen around the Country Club as far as Irene Fitzgibbons knows."

"What about at Sunny Days retirement community?"

"I'll be tackling that tomorrow with my deputies."

"Mavis Anderson would be the best person to help you out with introductions."

"That's not how we do things."

"I'm just saying, she knows every person who lives there and everyone who goes in or comes out."

He grimaced. "That's what I'm worried about—getting back out."

She snorted. "Mavis might be a gossip, but her heart is in the right place."

"I know. I wish I had more patience, but often I'm simply in a hurry."

"Sometimes people like Mavis need you not to be."

He winced. "Ouch. I'll do my best to remember that. How about we talk about *us* some more?"

"You know, I think we are. Talking about what we're good at and passionate about, makes me realize how much we think alike."

He reached across the table and ran a finger down her cheek. "Which could lead to a second date?"

A shiver trailed down her body. "At the very least."

They smiled as they ate and talked about the twins. Several people acknowledged them, but they must have understood that this was a special moment because no one lingered, and they were able to enjoy the evening.

Maddie sipped her wine then placed her hands on the table. "I have a confession."

Ethan tilted his head. "Am I going to like it?"

She laughed at his worried expression. "Everything I say isn't necessarily challenging."

He leaned back. "We'll see. What would you like to confess?"

"I can't tell your nephews apart. Ever."

"You seem to manage quite well."

"I cheat. I wait for you to say something to one or the other of them, then I pick an article of clothing or a color that they're wearing. The trouble is I have to do this every time I see them. It's not cool and a little stressful."

Ethan had begun to laugh and now he was practically rolling around in his seat.

"Why is it so funny?"

"Because it's so obvious."

She was a little insulted. "It would be to you, since they're your nephews!"

"Aside from James being marginally less wild than Jesse, James has a cowlick right in the front. Quite a big one. I don't know how you could miss it."

"Really? I honestly haven't noticed. James, you say? Well thank you, Sheriff. That's going to make life a darn sight easier from now on." She finished the last of her fish and sat back with a satisfied smile.

"I'm so pleased to be of service. Would you like to dance?"

She screwed up her face. "I'm not good at it. In fact, the Girlz laugh at my attempts."

His mouth twitched. "I remember. But I didn't laugh then, so I won't laugh now. Besides, with this kind of dancing, you just hold on to me and we'll just sway a bit. No pressure."

"Sounds easy enough. I hope you don't regret it."

He laughed, took her hand and led her to the small floor where a few other couples danced to a slow song. Ethan was right, they did nothing more than sway, and she felt comfortable in his arms. He smelled divine, and she could feel his muscles bunch under his shirt as they moved.

When they were done and with neither wanting dessert, Ethan drove her home. Very slowly. The moon was out in full and made the lake twinkle and ripple with light until they hit the rise of a hill. Then it was dark, apart from the lights from the town creating a soft glow ahead of them in the distance.

The silence was comfortable. When they arrived at the bakery, Ethan walked her to the door. There was no need for coyness as he took her in his arms. They'd both been waiting for this moment. It didn't disappoint.

He tucked her hair behind her head as he leaned down. "I hope we get to have many more nights like this."

"Me too." Her breath caught. Then he was kissing her.

Like the dance, it was long and leisurely. She sighed when he stepped back, feeling the cold air between them.

He ran a finger down her cheek. "I better go now, otherwise I might never leave."

She nodded, incapable of speaking but knowing that, if she did, it would be to ask him to stay.

"See you tomorrow." He kissed her forehead and went

back down the path, turning at the gate for one last look at her.

Maddie floated into the kitchen. It felt official. They were a couple for the second time, and she could see no dream or ambition that couldn't include the handsome Sheriff.

Chapter Eleven

Maddie and Laura walked to the gallery on Monday, leaving Luke to close up and finish the cleaning. It wouldn't be for long, and he was always happy to help out. Luckily, the bakery was traditionally quieter on Mondays too.

Suzy drove herself, since the school she was principal of was across town, and there wouldn't be a great deal of time between finishing there and getting to the Gallery to fill in for her mom.

Maddie confessed, "Apart from the other day I hadn't been here since I came back to Maple Falls."

Suzy tutted. "That was months ago."

"I know, but I have been a little occupied," she offered lamely.

Angel gave her a wink. "Yes, opening a shop and solving crimes will keep you busy."

Maddie narrowed her eyes. "Stop with the 'solving crimes', already. I've simply been looking into a few discrepancies."

"Ah-huh. You're forgetting how much Gran loves to tell

the stories of your recent brushes with some nasty criminals and how you just happened to be with Ethan when Owen was found."

Maddie made a rude noise. "I'm sure the town can find other things to gossip about, and Owen's death is not something to make light of."

"No one's doing that, Sugar. It is a tragedy."

Angel was contrite and Maddie put an arm around her shoulder, thinking it best to move the conversation to where it should be. The paintings. She turned to Suzy. "Okay, show us the best stuff you have."

"Are you talking money, or what I think is a better product?"

"Both." Maddie shrugged, not really appreciating the difference.

"This is Nicholas Brack's last work. His portrayal of sunset over the lake is beautiful and the mountains behind are just as imposing as they are in real life."

"Wow. You even sound like you know what you're talking about," Maddie teased.

"Rude. Listening to my mom, who has a degree in fine arts, describe the works to her customers may have rubbed off a little." Suzy grinned.

"With everything you do for the school and the community, I don't know how you find the time to work here."

"I only come in the odd days when Mom needs a break. Dad will come in if she's desperate, but that is totally a last resort."

"I can't imagine him in here." Angel smiled affectionately at the thought of her friend's father.

Laura put down a sculpture of a police officer which looked suspiciously like Rob Jacobs.

"Why is that?" she asked.

Suzy gave a wry grin. "You know the saying a bull in a china shop?"

Maddie and Angel laughed while Laura nodded.

"That's my dad. Plus, he doesn't have patience with tire kickers. He's not a salesperson and can be a bit abrupt."

"You sell tires? In here?" Angel looked around her.

Suzy frowned as if she wasn't sure to believe her naivety. "It means browsers. People who have no idea what they want and usually want it for next to nothing."

Angel arched an elegant eyebrow. "Well, I think it's a weird thing to say about someone buying art."

Maddie was listening to them, but she was also looking at the pieces on display. She wasn't a connoisseur of art in any way, but like Suzy, she knew what she liked. Some of the paintings were so realistic she felt drawn right into them. Others left her cold. She had no idea what they represented. Abstract was not her thing. She suddenly noticed a blank wall in the corner by the door that led out the back to the lunchroom and a small washroom. She hadn't noticed it when she came in with Ethan. A mark where a painting had hung was evident.

"Where's this picture, Suzy?"

"I'm not sure. It probably sold recently, and Mom hasn't replaced it yet. She has a stack of pictures in that corner, waiting for room to be displayed. Help yourself if you want to look through them. The stand holds them individually and they're quite safe."

Suzy was right. Each picture was housed in a separate space, like a concertina file, only a hundred times bigger and made of wood. She was able to flick through each one easily enough despite the weight of some of the larger ones which were already framed.

She came to the last one and felt something sticky on

her fingertips. It looked like paint. She sniffed them. It smelled like paint. As she carefully lifted the unframed picture out of its slot, she noticed a smear in one corner. She didn't believe she'd touched it there.

"Suzy? You know how you said I couldn't hurt these?"

Horrified, Suzy ran across the room. "Don't tell me you've ripped one?"

"Not exactly." Maddie held up her fingers. "I'm really sorry, but I've smeared the paint."

"That's impossible. Mom doesn't take any works that aren't dry. It would mean they had just been finished, and that would never happen in case it got damaged."

Maddie took a step back so Suzy could inspect the painting. Pulling it out carefully, the sheen of the damp area was more noticeable, and Suzy carried it to a large desk which was used to pack the art. She bent over it and made a few noises that Maddie was familiar with. Maddie waited, cleaning her fingers on a towel, then tapping them in her impatience. Suzy sent a glare her way, and Maddie clasped her hands in front of her.

"You're right about the damp corners of the painting. I wonder who the artist is? Goodness, the signature is E Wilson."

Maddie leaned over her. "You sound excited."

"She's a wonderful artist. Or, I should say, was."

"She's dead?"

"Yes, and before you go all super sleuth on me, it was years ago from natural causes. You probably haven't heard of her because it would only be in the last five years that her work was uncovered and lauded for being ahead of its time. She was Nicholas Brack's wife."

"Really? It's a nice painting of the mountains and the lake, but I wouldn't call it amazing."

"There are thousands who would disagree with you. The price for them has skyrocketed, so Mom's lucky to have one to hand. Perhaps that was her intention for the blank corner of the gallery. It bestows pride of place, showcasing the picture by itself so the eye isn't drawn elsewhere."

Maddie wasn't sure what to say about all that information. Dissecting it wasn't going to help her one bit, although she was sure it made sense, otherwise Suzy wouldn't be so delighted with her find. "What do you make of the wet paint?"

"I'll mention it to Mom, but this is highly irregular." She pointed to the corner of the smudged painting. "The colors fit with the rest of it, otherwise I'd be inclined to suggest another one had rubbed off on it. Except, that wouldn't make sense either, since like I said, we don't ever get any that aren't dry. I don't want to touch any more of it, but the other top corner looks a little wet too."

They studied the painting, but, apart from those two corners, nowhere else seemed affected.

Maddie could see that this bothered Suzy a great deal and thought that Ethan might also be interested in a painting, recently done, by a dead woman.

"Can I take a picture of it?"

Suzy nodded. "I don't see why not, if you promise you won't make a copy in your secret basement?"

Maddie laughed. "I wish I was talented enough to be tempted ... or had a secret basement for that matter."

Suzy waved her away. "Please! Your talents as a baker are just as artistic and far more important than a fresh painting masquerading as an older one."

She bit her lip as if she had said something wrong, but Maddie didn't pursue it. She took the photo with her phone then went back to the others who were now crowded around a set of handcrafted serving plates. A different view of the lake graced each one, and they were gorgeous.

Maddie would have loved one or all of them for her catering, but she saw the price and tamped down that idea before it could get any traction.

Suzy came over to the group, still looking worried, but trying to hide it. Maddie imagined, whatever was going on here, it didn't bode well for the gallery.

"Do you think the painting's a copy?" Laura asked.

"I can't think why Mom would buy one if it was, but I won't know for certain until I speak to her."

"If it is a copy, does that mean it's a forgery?"

"Mom wouldn't be involved in anything like that," Suzy hedged. "I think it's time to lock up, and I've got reports to write for school tomorrow."

Maddie stole a look at her watch. They had been there less than an hour. Cora kept traditional nine to five hours. Suzy must be really upset if she was closing early. But they left her to it and wandered back to the bakery.

"I don't like this business at all," Maddie said as they stood by her gate.

"Did I miss something?" Angel asked.

"The painting in Cora's gallery is not what it should be."

"But Suzy said it wasn't a forgery."

"No, she didn't."

Angel frowned while she tried to put it all together. Then she shook her head.

"Suzy wouldn't lie to us."

"She wasn't lying because she doesn't know for sure. She's protecting her mom by protecting the gallery and its reputation."

"Oh. How can we help her without making everyone think Cora is doing something illegal?" Angel bit her lip.

"I don't think we can, but Ethan might be able to."

"Yes. He can be discrete. Not that you aren't." Laura's cheeks reddened.

Maddie shook her head at her friends. They were as eager to help as she was even if they didn't approve of some of her methods.

Angel hugged her. "Then we'll let you deal with him. Good luck and call us if we can help in any way."

"Don't worry about that. I've learned my lesson about keeping Ethan in the dark about anything I'm planning."

"Sure you have." Angel grinned as she went two doors up to her salon and her own apartment.

Laura waved at both of them and went home to the cottage and Gran.

As Maddie got to the door, an orange paw reached out and grabbed the bottom of her pants. A squeal died in her throat. She might never get used to Big Red's tactics. He growled a little then curled around her legs as though he had just been saying hi.

"That is no way to greet me. I'm sorry for leaving you behind, but you were sleeping so soundly, I didn't think you'd notice."

He gave her a disdainful look but waited for her to open the door. He wouldn't lower himself to use the cat door when someone was on hand to let him in. Plus, it was nearly dinner time, which meant she was required to stay in his sight until his bowl was full.

Chapter Twelve

Ethan had been in another town all day Monday, and she knew he would be tired so hadn't phoned him last night about the painting, even though she had been itching to. But as soon as the sun came up, she sent him a text and was pleased to see him not long after.

He came through the door of the kitchen with barely a knock, took off his hat, and kissed her cheek. The twinkle in his eye let her know he would have liked to do better but a) he was in uniform and b) they had an audience.

Laura and Luke gave him a smile and said hello, but Big Red looked decidedly put out with Ethan's proximity. In fact, he reached out a paw from where he was crouched just inside the door and gave Ethan a whack on the ankle.

"He's letting you know you're out of order, Sheriff," Laura said, blushing and quickly turned back to frosting a cake.

Maddie often had a twinge of awkwardness around Laura when Ethan was there. She hoped one day that Laura could let it go that Maddie knew of her feelings for Ethan. As far as Maddie was concerned, it was in the past and didn't matter anymore, but her friend was still a little fragile around personal topics. With over-the-top parents like hers it was no wonder she had deeply embedded issues.

Ethan was, of course, oblivious to Laura's pink cheeks. He greeted both her and Luke in his usual friendly, relaxed way. Luke was still a little tentative around him, which she imagined might take some time to get over. Everyone had their story.

When her staff returned to work, Maddie nodded to the alcove, and Ethan followed her along with Big Red. Her protector jumped onto her chair at the small desk, pretending he wasn't aware of anyone aside from Maddie.

She pulled out her phone. "I need to show you this picture. I took it of a painting at the gallery. It was in a crate with many others. This was painted by a famous artist who is dead, but the painting is damp on the top corners."

"Damp?" he asked quietly as he enlarged the picture.

She nodded. "Wet oil paint. I got some of it on my fingers."

"I'll check it out myself, but was there any way moisture could have gotten in?

"I shouldn't think so. The stand that the paintings are in is like a big open crate made of wood, with sliding trays inside so you can flip the pictures. I never thought to look at the ceiling, but the gallery is pristine, and Cora likes to keep it that way. If there was a leak it would be dealt with quickly, and I'm sure she would have noticed if any paintings were affected."

He nodded. "I'll head over there now and talk to Cora. Suzy is knowledgeable, but no one knows as much about the stock and value of the art as her mother."

"I agree, but can I show you something else first?" She ignored his raised eyebrow and opened her laptop. "I googled the artist. Here she is. She passed away five years ago. Since then, her painting prices have gone through the roof. Look, this one sold recently for one hundred thousand dollars."

It was another landscape in the pastel colors E Wilson obviously liked to use.

Ethan whistled as he scrolled the page. "She painted so many."

"I know. Even prints of them go for several thousand."

"Wow. Anything else?"

"I think that's enough to keep you busy for now," she said with a twinkle in her eye.

He looked around, suddenly aware that they could not be seen from here.

"Actually, I've thought of something else."

His voice was husky, and hers became a little breathy as they gazed at each other.

"Yes, Sheriff?"

He pulled her into his arms and kissed her long and hard, so that her knees trembled. Whilst unexpected, it was certainly not unwanted, and she returned the kiss.

Her eyes shot open when she heard steps.

"Oh! Excuse me." Laura backed hurriedly away.

"It's okay," Maddie called after her. "Ethan was just leaving."

He coughed. "Yes, I was. You all have a good day."

He slipped on his hat as he went out the door, and Maddie gave him a small wave. She hadn't planned on their relationship escalating as it had. She hadn't planned on ever getting back with Ethan. But plans changed, and she was looking forward to spending more time with him once this case wrapped up.

"What did you need?" she asked Laura.

"Oh. This delivery will be late." She handed Maddie a piece of paper. "The company called with an apology."

Maddie blanched as she recognized the company she used for most of their supplies. "Of course, it's the delivery Owen was supposed to make. It certainly isn't their fault, but we'll need to do an inventory as soon as we can. I'd hate to run out of anything, and I noticed on Saturday that some ingredients are getting low."

"If we don't get too many customers, we could do it mid-morning, once we've stocked everything."

Maddie was pleased with the suggestion. "Excellent idea. You and I can do that while Luke handles the shop."

Luke agreed, and with that sorted, they managed to get everything on their schedules done in time to secure a window of time to do the inventory before the lunchtime rush.

The women went into the walk-in pantry. Maddie had a clipboard with all the ingredients listed alphabetically, and Laura called out amounts. Just as she thought, supplies were getting dangerously low on a couple of items but, provided they got a delivery in a day or two, they would be fine. Happier with that knowledge, she took Laura over to the schedule board to make a few adjustments for tomorrow, just in case.

"We did that in record time."

"Well, you are very organized." Laura grinned.

"I'm taking that as a compliment and not as a comment on my compulsive disorder."

Laura's eyebrows reached her hairline. "Do you really have that?"

"I'm pretty sure I do, and Angel would certainly agree." She laughed at herself. It was just the way she was, and she'd likely never change. She loved being organized but had tried to tame her fear of not getting around to everything she wanted to achieve each day.

Laura giggled and Maddie seized the opportunity.

"I want to talk to you about something, but I don't want it to offend you."

"Sounds serious. Have I done something wrong?" Laura's voice shot up a couple of octaves.

"No, I don't think it is, and you most certainly haven't done anything wrong. It's not about work."

Laura grimaced. "Just say it."

Maddie put a hand on her arm. "Do you still have feelings for Ethan?"

"I never ..." Laura gulped. "Oh, that's a lie. I did have feelings for him, but he only has eyes for you. He is one heck of a man and you deserve him. That's all there is to it. I've moved on. It's just embarrassing that you know about it."

"Are you sure?"

Laura gave her a steady look. "I'm sure." Then she grinned. "As long as you don't mind me admiring him from afar?"

"I'm not blind to his appeal—obviously," Maddie snorted. "I can also see the appeal to other women, which is why I felt the need to clear the air. I didn't want it to come between us."

"Because I saw you kiss? I'm a big girl Maddie. I'm not jealous. Maybe a little envious, but I'm happy for the two of you."

"Laura, you have no idea how relieved I am."

"Can I get some help here?" Luke called from the shop.

"I'll go. I'm sure you have a list or two to make for the next delivery." Laura winked cheekily.

Maddie sat down at her desk with a lighter heart and

Big Red jumped up on the desk and squeezed himself onto her lap. He gave her a wise look and curled himself into a very large ball. Sometimes things had to be brought out into the open, and sometimes they were best left unsaid. She was glad that her talk with Laura had turned out to be the former.

Naturally, her thoughts returned to Laura being over Ethan. Did it have something to do with Deputy Rob Jacobs?

This was another mystery, but one that would be sweet if it got solved in the way she hoped.

Chapter Thirteen

E than called Tuesday night to say that he would be out of town for a few days and he would see her when he got back. He added that Maddie should behave herself. He sounded serious. She said she would try, but things had a way of cropping up when he wasn't around, so she couldn't promise.

Wednesday proved to be one of those times.

Behind the counter, she had served Jed Clayton with his usual order of coffee and a slice of the cake of the day—in this case, chocolate gateau—when Suzy's mom entered. After the formalities, Jed took a seat while Cora studied the display case.

"Are you looking for anything in particular?" Maddie asked.

"I've come for some of your cakes. I have a potential client coming in for a private showing tonight. I don't know what he might like. I'll have wine and cheese, but he might prefer coffee or tea, in which case, I'd like to offer them something bite-sized to accompany that?"

"I'm sure I could cut down some slices or make you something special if you have any suggestions?"

"I don't have a clue, so anything would be great. Sorry about the short notice, but he only rang an hour ago. The things he's interested in are not cheap, so if you could do something special, I'd be so grateful." Cora was buzzing with excitement.

"It's no problem at all. I'm sure I can think of something. When did you want them?"

"He should be there about seven, so any time before then?"

"Sure. I'll drop them off if you like, so you don't have to worry about picking them up?" Maddie offered.

"I'd appreciate that. To be honest, I feel a little flustered. Silly really since I've dealt with a few famous people, but they're artists. This feels so different."

"I'm sure you will be just fine. Should I cater for just the two of you?"

"That's a good point. He said there would likely be one or two other people, but they weren't buying, whatever that means."

"Perhaps he's bringing family?"

Cora frowned. "I really don't have a clue. I should have asked more questions, but he knew what he wanted and was quick to get off the call."

"Hopefully that means you'll get a decent sale." Maddie's skin prickled with worry over Cora being on her own with a stranger wanting to look around the gallery where Owen had been hanging around prior to his death.

"I do hope so. With winter coming I need a few good sales. I'd better get back to the gallery. Dan's looking after it while I run my errands, and he's not exactly a great salesperson."

Maddie laughed. Suzy had said the same thing about her father, but Mr. Barnes had always been a sweetheart when Maddie was around him. She couldn't imagine him as anything more than a big teddy bear of a man.

Laura was out front serving the coffee and apple pie Mr. Clayton had ordered, but when she returned, Maddie told her about Cora's request. Since she had such an affinity for baking, Maddie was pushing Laura into a more senior role and liked to include her in decisions.

"What do you think would be good for this order?"

Laura looked through the display case. "We still have the lunch group to get through, so I don't think we'll be able to take anything from the shop without leaving us short on baked goods. Besides, if they're fancy people, then perhaps we should make something to suit." She put a hand to her mouth as she turned to Maddie. "I didn't mean that what you sell isn't first class."

Maddie waved her apology away. "I know what you meant, and I had the same thoughts. Let's rustle up some rum balls, mini fruit tarts and salmon blinis with creme fraise?"

Laura couldn't hide her relief. Pale skin warmed with flushed cheeks of excitement. "They sound lovely. Luke and I can manage the order if you want?"

"Great. I'll carry on with some paperwork, and you delegate the jobs. I'll pull out the recipes and be close by if you need me."

"I'll go tell Luke."

The young man happened to come from the kitchen just then with a tray of fresh raspberry-filled doughnuts.

"Tell me what?" he asked.

"We have a new order, and you're making rum balls."

"Really? I've never made those. It'll be something different."

Maddie laughed. As much as they all liked baking, it was good to be able to tackle different recipes, and she understood the urge to always be learning.

"I'm happy to be the guinea pig if you need someone to sample them," Mr. Clayton called out from over his paper.

"If you're still here by the time they're made, the job is yours," Maddie answered then went to her alcove and pulled out the recipes. She'd have to make sure she had enough ingredients. If there was no delivery tomorrow, she'd have to make the trip into Destiny to pick up supplies.

By the end of the day they'd made everything Maddie promised Cora, and Luke and Laura had gone home.

With Big Red fed, Maddie put everything on the counter to take to the gallery. She was using her best platters to serve the delicate finger food, and she carefully loaded the back of Honey with them, laying them inside aluminum trays she had purchased for this sort of thing. She wore tidy black trousers and a white shirt just in case Cora wanted her to serve.

Arriving at six thirty, she had to knock at the back door since the shop was locked up. She'd had to park in the same spot that the infamous van had used, and a prickle ran across her arms as she thought about Owen's murder. Since it was getting dark, especially between the two buildings, she wished Cora would hurry and let her in. Since she was expected, she'd assumed that one door would be open, but had to knock several times before Cora opened the door.

The usually bubbly woman was white-faced and jittery. "I'm so glad it's you, dear. Come on in."

"Is something wrong, Mrs. Barnes?"

Cora forced a laugh. "I'm being silly. I thought I heard

noises and gave myself a fright. That's why both doors are locked. I was just checking the bathroom windows. Now you're here, I'll unlock the front door for my customers."

The shaking of her voice made Maddie think her friend's mother wouldn't be happy on her own for any length of time, regardless of whether or not her fear was warranted.

"With the park so close, you've probably heard a lot of funny noises and, since you're not usually at work at this time of night, they sound worse than they are."

"You could be right," the small woman said uncertainly.

"How about I stay with you until your customers have gone?"

Cora let out an exaggerated sigh. "Would you? I didn't like to ask, but I would be grateful. Suzy has one of her meetings tonight otherwise she would have been here, and Dan is in Destiny visiting his brother overnight. You know how he loves his football?"

She did indeed. Mr. Barnes was crazy about the Oregon Ducks and it wasn't just football he followed. Any sport could easily lure him away from having to work in the gallery. He had recently left the army and was finding it difficult to settle into his retirement.

"I'm happy to keep you company. And I thought I could serve the drinks and food, so you don't have to bother."

"You're such a dear. It's very kind of you. I thought the food could go on this small table in the corner. I have white wine in the fridge and a bottle of red to open. The coffee and tea are on the counter in the back."

Maddie smiled reassuringly. "I'll find everything. You leave this to me and carry on with what you need to do."

"I gave the place a thorough clean today, but I'd like to lay out the paintings they specifically asked to see. I'll ask them whether they would like a drink when they arrive. If you could see to that, then I'll give you a nod when I think it would be a good time for refreshments. Probable once they are done browsing."

"Sounds like a good plan."

They went to do their allotted tasks. Maddie quickly laid the table with her plates of food and also the cheese and crackers Cora had indicated. She was out the back, opening a bottle of red wine, when the bell above the door sounded.

Creeping to the doorway, for no other reason than her senses were on high alert after the issue of strange noises had been raised, she could see a burly man had entered. He wore a dark suit accompanied by a darker scowl and took a moment to look around the room.

Before Cora could say anything, he opened the door for another man to enter. This one was much shorter. He also wore a dark suit, but had his hair slicked back. He had the air of someone with a big personality and was noticeably friendlier, although his smile seemed overbright.

The bigger man shut the door once more, but not before Maddie noted that a third man stood outside by a dark sedan. He wasn't in a suit, which was the only thing she could really see from where she was. Was she being para-noid to feel as though she was in a gangster movie?

"Good evening and welcome." Cora smiled warmly.

The bigger man ignored her outstretched hand and without replying positioned himself to the side of the gallery that held no windows. From there he could see the entire room and out onto the street. The small man came forward with enthusiasm, compensating for the other man's rudeness.

He shook her hand, patting it with his other. "It's a pleasure to meet you, Mrs. Barnes, thank you for opening up tonight. I really appreciate it."

Cora was a tactile person and she loved the gesture, but it made Maddie cringe. Sleazy was the word for it—especially the way his eyes gave a longer than acceptable glance over Suzy's mom. That was all kinds of wrong.

"It's Mr. Smith, isn't it? And please, call me Cora. It's my pleasure. You said you were interested in the latest paintings I have from E Wilson?"

"That's right." He nodded.

"Unfortunately, I only have the one and it may be slightly damaged like I told you when you called. Luckily my daughter found it before mold could set in."

"May I see it?"

"Of course. I have it waiting just over here." She led him to the large counter, and the other man followed. "Cora Barnes." She held out her hand to him. "Would either of you like a drink while you look?

To Maddie, who'd had to slip out into the gallery to be able to see them, and had hidden behind a large easel, it seemed as though the big man didn't want to have anything to do with Cora. It could have been the scowl the other man sent his way that changed his mind because eventually he did take her hand. But the big man still didn't look happy about having to make the exchange.

"We'd rather get on with seeing the painting," he said in a firm, deep voice.

Cora frowned at the handshake which made her knuckles whiten with the pressure and Maddie was about to go to her aid when he released her.

Taking a step away from him, Cora turned slightly to Mr. Smith. She pointed at the counter. "Well, this is it. I can't explain what happened, but we found small damp sections on the painting—the top corners. We investigated, but no other paintings have been affected. I'm sorry it's not in perfect condition, and would naturally reduce the price."

He shook his head. "Oh, I don't think we need worry about it. These things happen, and I know her work never fails to exact a good amount, no matter the condition. I'll take this one and look at some of your other pictures while I'm here. If you don't mind?"

"Certainly. Feel free to browse. When you're ready, my assistant will bring out refreshments."

"Your assistant?" the big man growled.

He scanned the room until he spied Maddie in the corner. She came out from behind the easel to stand in front of a large painting with the bottle of red wine in her hand. She tried to look professional, but her knees shook a little. If necessary, the bottle could be used as a weapon, she supposed. But she had no illusions that she was a physical match for this man as he crossed the room to her with a speed that belied his size.

Mr. Smith's voice hardened. "I heard that your husband worked here sometimes, I didn't realize you had other help."

Cora and Maddie shared a look. Something funny was definitely going on, and she could see by the fear in her eyes that Cora was finally on the same page. Neither of them were comfortable about being here with the dangerous-looking men. This had nothing to do with a vivid imagination.

Cora followed the big man. "Oh, I have several assistants, and my husband should be here any minute."

"Didn't he go to Destiny?" the big man asked and received a glare from Mr. Smith.

"Why yes. How did you know that?" Cora asked.

"You must have told me when I rang earlier, and I

shared the information with Mr. Chance," Mr. Smith interjected reasonably.

Cora shook her head. "I don't believe so, but no matter. He was going to watch a football game with his brother who's taken sick. That's why he's coming back tonight after all," she explained reasonably.

Smith shrugged. "I'm sure it's not relevant for me to buy some of your lovely art. It's simply that I prefer to do so without an audience." He turned away and went back to looking through the crate.

"I understand completely. Let me know if you need anything."

Cora went behind her counter and shuffled papers while Maddie did her best not to look at Chance as she toyed with the plates and glasses.

Chance moved back to Smith's side and they whispered furtively as Smith flicked through the paintings.

Cora coughed to draw her attention. "Perhaps you could get the rest of the refreshments ready?"

Maddie reluctantly went out the back to make coffee in the small kitchen area and had been there barely a few seconds when Chance came through the doorway.

"I'm sorry, this is a private area," her voice shook.

He ignored her, so she pretended outwardly that he wasn't there and prepared the drinks, knowing that this had been a small, and perhaps the only, opportunity to call someone. Inside, she was a quivering mess. Cora had lied about Dan coming back, and if Maddie didn't believe it, then, more than likely, neither did the two men.

"Here," she thrust a tray of rum balls and tarts at him. "Make yourself useful."

The giant was not expecting that, and he wasn't

amused, but he followed her into the gallery with one tray while she took another with coffee and cups.

Cora came towards her in relief. "Thank you, Maddie. Gentlemen, would you care for a drink and something to eat?"

"That's very good of you, Mrs. Barnes—Cora. I'm not sure we have the time, do we Mr. Chance?"

"What a shame. Maddie is a wonderful baker and I hate to waste all this food."

Maddie touched Cora's arm and spoke quietly, although loud enough for the men to hear.

"I meant to tell you when I got here but we were so busy. Sheriff Tanner said he would stop by soon, and I'm sure he'd love to take the leftovers."

"Did he?"

Maddie frowned at Cora and luckily she took the hint.

"That's lovely. I wanted to see him anyway."

"Why would the sheriff be coming here?" Chance narrowed his eyes.

Maddie swung around. He was too close to be anything but threatening, and Maddie held the tray between them like a barrier. "He's investigating a death. You must have heard about it?"

Chance frowned, his dark eyes studying her. "No, we're not from around here."

"Where are you from?" Maddie bit her lip. She shouldn't be antagonizing him.

"Portland."

She gave him a fake smile. "It's lovely there."

Mr. Smith handed Cora his credit card. "Yes, it is. Actually, we need to get going. We have a long drive."

Cora took the platinum card. "I'll package the painting and send it to you if you'd like to leave me your address."

He shook his head. "If you don't mind, I'll take it now."

His pleasantness seemed to be waning.

Cora sniffed. "Yes, of course. Did you want anything else?"

He pointed to the others Cora had displayed on the counter. "I'll take these two as well. I have my eye on another couple of pieces, so I'll be in touch when I decide."

He looked at Maddie as he said this, causing a chill to run through her. Even if the transaction was legitimate, she knew that these two men were not.

Maddie helped Cora package all three paintings and she saw the prices as Cora made up invoices. The other two paintings were a fraction of the price of the E Wilson one. It didn't make sense. If they were connoisseurs of art, why would they choose arguably lesser works?

Smile back in place, Smith shook Cora's hand then held the door open for Chance, who carried the paintings out to their car. The third man must have been behind the wheel, since the car started as soon as Chance stowed the art in the back. They had barely closed their doors before the car shot off into the night.

Cora quickly turned the lock and leaned on the wall, putting a hand to her chest. "I didn't imagine that, did I?"

Maddie ran to the counter and grabbed a pen and began to scribble on a piece of paper.

"If you mean the threatening innuendo, then, no, you certainly didn't imagine it. Something's going on and I'd bet a week's worth of baking that it's got nothing to do with wanting a nice painting or two."

Cora gasped. "Ethan didn't mention anything to me when he stopped by yesterday on his way out of town. Is he really coming by tonight?"

"No, he's in Destiny. I just said that so we wouldn't appear to be two vulnerable women."

"Good thinking. With the increase in interest this last year, I had intended to organize more evening showings. I couldn't do it now."

"I'd definitely put that on hold for now. In fact, I'm going to give Deputy Jacobs a call and see if he wouldn't mind stopping by here tonight."

"Really? Do you think it's necessary to call him out now that they've gone?"

"Ethan would expect me to. The longer you leave these things the more likely it is to forget important facts."

Maddie was already keying in numbers. It was the right thing to do, and Rob was only too happy to come by, which implied that he agreed even if she hadn't gone into all the details. When she was done, she began to clear the untouched plates and glasses.

"Why did they want a painting that was damaged? And why take the other two?" Cora began to pace. "The three are nothing alike and the smaller ones belong to relatively new artists."

Maddie nodded. "I wondered about that too. I wish we could have taken a better look at those before we packaged them up. I don't mean to be rude, but they were quite bland."

"I would never say such a thing to the artists, and I believe in giving people a chance, but between us, I do agree. In fact, I didn't hold out much hope that they would ever sell. It made no sense that a connoisseur of art would want them."

"Did Ethan talk about anything else when you saw him?"

"Not really. He wanted to know more about Nicholas

Brack, so I gave him the address. He was also concerned about the state of the painting. There's that as well. I had every intention of dropping the price, but they scared me so much, I went with the original one. The payment was accepted."

Maddie couldn't help laughing at Cora and her self-satisfied look. "It's good that the night wasn't a complete failure, but I hope they don't come back."

Cora nodded. "Me too. I'd rather not have the money than go through all that anguish again."

They were walking into the kitchen when Maddie stopped.

"The last time I was in, there wasn't a painting in this corner, but I see you've got one there now." She pointed to the landscape in pale colors that didn't do justice to Maple Falls.

"It's hard to let the works go that you fall in love with and that was a particularly lovely E. Wilson. This was the best I could find to replace it and it's nice enough, but not even close to her caliber." She sighed.

Maddie would have liked to have seen that earlier picture. They were packaging up the wasted food and even had a small glass of wine to temper their nerves when there was a knock at the back door and they both jumped.

"Who is it?" Maddie asked.

"Deputy Jacobs."

They let him in, and Cora explained everything in fine detail. Then Maddie handed him the piece of paper she had written on.

"Their license plate number? You're a star, Maddie."

She colored a little. "I can't emphasize how scary they were. It was the only thing I could think of." Then she remembered something else. "Credit cards!"

Startled, Cora took a step back.

"They paid by credit card?" Rob asked calmly.

"Mr. Smith did. Where's the register receipt Cora?"

Suzy's mom ran to the register and opened it. She pulled out a slip of paper and handed it to him.

"I'm going to head over to the station and see if we can trace either of these back to your men. Cora, I think you should go to Suzy's for the night. I can drop you off to the cottage to stay with Gran and Laura, Maddie."

"I can't imagine them being interested in a baker. I'll be fine at my place."

He was about to argue but could perhaps see her determination.

"Okay. Please make sure you lock up."

"I will. If you don't want any of this food, Cora, I thought Rob could take it back to the station?"

"That's fine with me. If I take it with me tonight, I'd likely eat the lot."

Rob grinned. "I don't mind if I do, thank you ladies."

He had a gleam in his eye and Maddie didn't like the chances that his fellow deputies would get much of the bounty.

Rob helped her take the plates to Honey, then walked Cora to her car parked out on the main street, saw her off safely, and did the same for Maddie.

It was quite dark on Plum Place when she arrived home. The trees across the road swished in the breeze, making her skin prickle. Opening the garage, she made a promise to herself to put more lights out here. With her keys in her hand—one placed between two fingers as Grandad had taught her, in case of an attack—she ran to the kitchen door, let herself in and, with relief, locked it behind her.

Two eyes stared at her from the stairs, and she gulped

down a squeal. She knew those eyes. Still, she put the light on and knelt down so Big Red could welcome her home properly.

It was easy to be brave in front of Cora and Rob, but who was she kidding? That one scary evening. She buried her face in the orange fur and waited until her heart settled. Then she went upstairs with her guard cat, deliberately leaving the light on and taking her laptop with her.

Forcing her mind to think about work was one way to quiet her questioning mind, but it wasn't working this time. So she and Big Red crawled under the blankets with her phone.

After everything that had happened tonight it was worth a call to Ethan even if Rob had already spoken to him.

Chapter Fourteen

Ethan had been very glad she had called him last night. He was interested and worried in equal measure. Glad that she and Cora were safe, he also praised her for calling Rob and hoped to be back in Maple Falls this morning so that he could talk to her face to face.

As much as hearing his voice made her feel a little better, Maddie hadn't slept well. Thoughts of the innuendos and the purchasing of random paintings and what it all meant ran around inside her head. When she'd finally had enough of tossing and turning, she got up and began to bake. Keeping her hands busy and her mind focused on something else nearly always helped settle her.

Today it wasn't doing so well. She put the bread dough to rise and a chocolate cake in the oven, then went to the alcove to fire up her laptop.

A key in the door startled her, but it was only Gran. Maddie could see that she had heard about last night by the intense look on her usually sunny face.

"I see you locked the door. At least I can be grateful for that."

"Who told you?"

"Cora called this morning to make sure you were okay. She started off by talking about coming on our next community center trip and how she'd need to ask Dan to work in the Gallery."

"And?"

"And I knew she was trying hard not to tell me something. Eventually, she let slip that you and she had a couple of dodgy clients last night to deal with."

"They weren't boy scouts, that's for sure."

"I don't know how you manage to get into these situations, granddaughter."

"Me either, but I couldn't leave her alone with them. Cora was scared."

Gran sighed. "I guess not. What am I saying? I wouldn't have left her alone either. So now we have a dead body and odd happenings at the gallery. Anything else you'd hoped to keep from me?"

Maddie was reluctant to impart any further knowledge. She didn't want Gran to worry any more than she was, but the look Gran was giving her meant there was only one way out of this. She had to tell her everything and trust it wouldn't be detrimental to her nearly seventy-year-old health.

"I haven't told anyone else, and Ethan wants to keep this quiet for now. Owen was definitely gassed with carbon monoxide. The tests should be back if that was the actual cause of death."

"Well, that's not really news, is it? Most of the retirement community saw and heard that it was likely. What else?"

"He was hit in the head. Probably the same pipe that was used to funnel the gas into the van."

"Nasty. What are you doing on the computer?" Gran asked suspiciously.

"I'm looking for any information regarding Nicholas Brack."

"Nicholas? Why him?"

"I hear he's been a bit of a recluse for some time, but one of the men at Cora's wanted any of his works. Even one that was damaged."

"Poor Nicholas. He had a bad time of it when one of his works had such terrible reviews that it was said he'd lost his talent and he was hounded about it in the press. It gave him severe anxiety, and I don't believe he's painted another thing since."

Maddie slapped her forehead. "Why do I bother researching anything when I could simply ask you?"

Gran shrugged. "What can I say? People talk to me about most things, including each other. Although I try not to gossip, it never hurts to be aware of what the people around you are feeling and, in some instances, doing."

Maddie knew this was true. There was hardly a person in town who hadn't chosen to spill their life story to Gran at one time or another. Unsure what else there was to know, she typed Nicolas Brack's name into the search engine. It showed his works over the years that had won him accolades. They were amazing country scenes, but he'd painted nothing new for six years. A couple of articles came up about the painting which had been lambasted by art critics across the country five years ago.

It couldn't be a coincidence, could it? Gran said he had anxiety, but his wife had also died around that time. Were these things connected?

Next, she looked up the painters of the two that Mr. Smith—as if that was his real name!—had also purchased. The painters, like Cora had said, were relative newcomers, and had both done small showings in Destiny, but were certainly not on the most desirable works list. The dreadful 'why' plagued her more than ever as she saw some of their works online. Not the ones in the gallery, but very similar.

Gran tutted. "Those are truly awful. Or am I an old fuddy-duddy with no taste?"

Maddie laughed. "Cora doesn't think they're very good and neither do I. I guess there's no accounting for taste."

Luke and Laura arrived then, and she closed the lid. It was enough that Gran knew for now. No sense in worrying everyone. She would delve into it more with Ethan, when he arrived.

She left the two interns to their work while she and Gran loaded up the oven with bread dough. By the time they had enough baked goods to fill up the display cases, the shop was open. Soon Mr. Clayton arrived for his usual coffee and was delighted with the fresh slice of chocolate cake Maddie presented to him.

"It's a new recipe, so the first slice is on the house."

He grinned. "I'm your guinea pig, is that what you're saying?"

"And a handsome one at that."

He roared with laughter. "I shan't be able to say a bad word against it now."

She snorted. "Don't think like that, otherwise I won't be able to give you samples anymore."

"Is that a threat young lady?"

"Who's threatening whom?" Ethan came through from the kitchen with Gran.

Maddie was ridiculously glad to see him and couldn't

help giving him a beaming smile. Mr. Clayton noticed and waggled his eyebrows at her.

"He's misbehaving, Sheriff," she teased.

"Is that a fact?"

"Not me, sir. It's this little lady who's a handful. Are you sure you can handle her?"

Maddie shook her head. "You're incorrigible."

"I'm sure going to try, Jed, but I won't promise. Maddie, can I have a word?"

"Gladly." She shook her finger at Jed as she left.

Jed's chuckle followed them as, by an unspoken agreement, they passed through the kitchen and headed upstairs. Once in her small sitting room, Ethan pulled her into his arms.

"You have no idea how long I've been waiting to kiss you again, Ms. Flynn," he said, looking into her eyes.

"I believe I do, Sheriff," she managed to answer, before his lips touched hers.

The kiss was warm and familiar with an edge to it that she understood. It was like coming home all over again. Safe and warm and … something else. A need she had tried to tamp down since she'd seen Ethan again last spring.

Reluctantly they pulled away but kept their arms around each other. Ethan stared at her in wonder and she knew right then that the feeling was mutual. She felt warm from head to toe as her heart kept up a steady tattoo.

Big Red wasn't as impressed. From the corner of her eyes she could see him sitting on the arm of the sofa, glaring at them. The good news was he hadn't bitten Ethan, something he was inclined to do if someone was touching Maddie in a way he didn't approve of. It might not seem that way, but she thought her large cat was warming to the prospect of having Ethan around more. Although, not quite as warm as Maddie.

"I was worried after your call last night."

"I'm sorry, I had a strong need to share what had happened."

"Don't be sorry. I'm glad you did, but I need to tell you something, only I don't want you to be angry about it."

She leaned back to study his troubled features. "I guess you'll just have to tell me so I can decide for myself."

He sighed. "I should have told you. Jacobs was keeping a watch on you and Cora."

"At the gallery?"

"Yes."

She chewed her bottom lip for a moment. "I can't be angry. I wish I'd known though. I might not have been as scared. Especially for Cora. She was so upset. I called Suzy to ask her about her mom, but her phone went to message. I hope she's okay?"

"I tried her too and, when I couldn't get ahold of her, I went to her apartment. She's fine but shaken about her mother and annoyed with herself for letting her phone die. Cora stayed the night and Dan should be home soon. Suzy said she'd come by on her lunch break."

There was a knock on the wall as Gran came up the stairs.

"Sorry to interrupt you two." She grinned knowingly at them. "Detective Jones is here."

The detective was close on her heals. "I got your message, Sheriff. Looks like we have ourselves another investigation that's proving to have more arms than an octopus."

Gran laughed. "I couldn't have said it better myself."

"Do you want to go somewhere private?" Ethan asked.

For the first time, Maddie witnessed the detective laugh. He appeared to be in very good spirits for someone who was in Maple Falls to solve a murder.

"I won't drag you away from Ms. Flynn or pretend that she doesn't already have the same information that we do."

Ethan looked uncomfortable. "I've been out of town on and off for a few days and things have been happening that are pertinent to the case, so I've been catching up with a few people."

"And Mrs. Flynn?"

Gran shrugged. "What can I say? I do know a lot of people in Maple Falls. Sometimes the information just spills from their mouths without me even asking."

Detective Jones raised an eyebrow. "I've heard the same thing from many hereabouts when I was interviewing them about the Owen Kirk case."

"Then you'll appreciate that we're trying to help, not interfere."

"And perhaps you can appreciate that knowing every-thing could lead to either or both of you being in danger?"

Gran nodded. "Maddie should be more careful, I grant you, but nobody would be interested in harming an old lady."

"Mrs. Flynn ..."

"Call me Gran."

"Ahhh, as much as I'd like to, I'm afraid it's not possible."

"Give it a try, young man. You'll be surprised how easy it is. Now, what were you saying?"

His mouth twitched. "I'm more worried about you. With your involvement at the community center and the retirement community, it's far more likely that you'll come into contact with the people we're tracking."

Gran's eyes widened. "Really? What people?"

Maddie sighed. Gran had tried many times to make Maddie take a step back on the cases she'd been involved in and now, here she was, as excited as Big Red near catnip.

"People I'd rather you stayed away from."

"I see. Well, I've got cakes in the oven, so I'll let you get on with your detective work and I'll bear what you've said in mind."

When she'd gone the detective turned to Maddie and Ethan.

"She didn't hear a word of it, did she?"

"She heard all right. I can't promise that it'll change anything. She can be stubborn," Maddie admitted.

Detective Jones smiled. He was much less formidable when that happened, which was perhaps why he didn't do it very often. A detective, like a sheriff, needed to have the credibility that seriousness conveyed. Fortunately, Ethan had not subscribed as heavily to that principle.

"I guess it runs in the family."

This was a statement rather than a joke and Maddie sniffed.

Detective Jones continued. "We have deputies out there keeping tabs on the men you met last night, thanks to your diligence in getting a license plate, but these men are clever and they're not going to be easy to catch in the act."

"Believe me, I understand how dangerous they are, and I'll keep a closer eye on Gran."

"I hope you do. Sheriff, I'd like to go over the crime scene again if you have time?"

They followed him down the stairs and Maddie saw them out. Gran was nonchalantly making frosting for her cooling cakes. Maddie didn't imagine that keeping an eye on her was going to be as easy as it sounded. She would need help, and Laura would be the perfect person since she lived with Gran.

Between the two of them they would know Gran's whereabouts most of the day. It would be when both Laura and Maddie were working, and Gran wasn't, that the biggest worry would be.

Which turned out to be that very afternoon.

Chapter Fifteen

Hands sticky with frosting for a birthday cake, Maddie pressed the speaker on her phone with the end of her palette knife.

"Hello?"

"Maddie? Do you have a moment?"

"Gran? Where are you? Are you okay?"

"Don't be silly, dear. I'm at Sunny Days, visiting Mavis."

"Oh. Good. I do have some time, now that the lunch rush is over."

"I thought so. Could you come by?"

Maddie got the distinct impression from Gran's edgy tone, that this wasn't a social invitation. "I'm on my way."

Laura cut off the call for her, then held her hand out for the knife. She'd been happy to keep tabs on Gran when she could and was just as worried about her as Maddie.

"I can finish that if you need to go now. It sounded important."

Maddie handed her the knife. "I thought so too. I wonder what she's got herself into?"

She washed her hands quickly and took off her apron. Leaving Laura and Luke to handle the bakery, she drove Honey to the Sunny Days as fast as she could.

Mavis had an apartment at the far end of the complex. Gran answered the door as soon as Maddie knocked and led her into the sitting room where Mavis sat on a floral couch looking puzzled.

"Mavis is bothered by strange noises coming from next door. She's known Mr. Langham for some time but hasn't seen him for days."

"Have you called the police, Mavis?"

"I really did mean to, but I wondered if I was imagining things."

Gran answered for her. "I haven't heard anything since I got here, but I did call Ethan before calling you. It went to his voice mail."

Maddie scratched her head. "Then I don't understand what I'm doing here?"

"Mr. Langham is away," Mavis informed her.

"You know that for sure?"

"I do. He goes out of town quite often and can be gone for several days at time. He left me a key so I could feed Rembrandt, his cat, because he wasn't sure how long he'd be gone. I'm too scared to go into his apartment."

"How about I take a look? It's probably Rembrandt, knocking over something. Big Red is always knocking things over when I'm out."

It didn't sound as though it was anything bad, especially if a cat was involved, so Maddie wasn't too worried.

"Would you?" Mavis was pleased.

"Do you think we should let Ethan know you're going in?" Gran asked.

"I'll send him a text." She proceeded to do just that. "I

know he's busy with Detective Jones today, but you're right that he'd want to know."

Maddie took the key from Mavis and went next door. The two older women hovered beside her as she knocked several times. She called his name, but there was no answer.

Putting the key in the lock, she turned it quickly and pushed the door hard. If there was anyone there, they would have a) left by the back door or b) waiting for her to enter.

Pausing for several seconds, she sidled along the wall until it opened out into a sitting room, identical in layout to Mavis's, but as different as was possible. The walls and ceiling were yellowed from cigarette smoke. Wallpaper curled at the edges in several spots. But the biggest difference was the presence of some stains—of various hues—on the carpet.

Quietly she walked through the apartment, not touching anything. No one was there, which was a huge relief. Then she heard a clatter from the kitchen. She poked her head around the corner to find a tabby licking at an empty bowl. It looked at her pointedly, then came to rub in between her ankles for attention, although more likely he was asking for food.

She picked him up and carried him through the sitting room and was on her way to give him to Mavis to feed when she noticed something on a side table by the couch. It was a baseball cap. The same kind that Owen had always worn. Coincidence? Perhaps. Thousands of these would be sold every year. But something about it was oddly familiar.

As she headed out the door, Ethan and Detective Jones pulled up outside in Ethan's sedan.

She dropped the cat into Mavis's arms. "I'll be back soon. I just want to show the sheriff and detective something."

"What did you find?" Mavis asked

"There's nobody there, so it's all safe, but perhaps you could keep Rembrandt until Mr. Langham comes home? He's very hungry."

"I guess I could do that," Mavis agreed, not overjoyed at being fobbed off.

Gran gave Maddie an understanding look and took Mavis into her apartment while Maddie led the detective and Ethan into Mr. Langham's place.

Ethan and Detective Jones were quiet while she told them why she had texted.

"Mavis heard sounds through the wall which was what alerted her that something was amiss in here. She thought it was maybe just the cat, but there was nothing broken or overturned when I came in."

"So, we don't really know if there has been a crime committed?" The detective didn't look impressed.

"No, we don't, except there's something else." She pointed to the cap and told them her suspicion about the owner.

The detective took a closer at it "There must be thousands of these in circulation. What makes you think it was Mr. Kirk's?"

"It's that logo, or rather, the top corner of it. There's a black mark, like a fingerprint in ash."

Detective Jones was surprised. "That's darn impressive. Why would you notice that?"

"Gran mentioned one day that she'd like to give it a clean for him, since he clearly loved it so much, but he was always in a rush."

"Anything else?"

"Not that I noticed. I didn't touch anything," she added.

"What about the back door? Locked or unlocked?"

"I didn't want to try it in case I wiped off prints."

The detective gave her an admiring glance before he pulled a glove from his pocket and pulled on the door handle. It opened with ease out onto a small courtyard.

The two men studied the grass around the area from their haunches, and Ethan pointed to the tread of a shoe headed away from the apartments across a small lawn which led to adjoining fields.

"At night a person could come and go around here and never be seen," Detective Jones stated.

"There is a security guard who swings by several times, but he takes care of the whole town and is employed by the council rather than this community," Ethan told him.

"We should speak to him, but I'm thinking whoever came in here took pains not to be seen."

"But didn't worry about being heard," Maddie added.

"Pardon?" The detective swung around to face her.

"The noises Mavis noticed?" she reminded him. "I suspect the cat is innocent after all."

"Hmmm. I guess we better go talk to her first."

"Please be gentle. She's naturally upset and will be more so if Mr. Langham is actually missing as a result of foul play."

"That's a step too far right now. We only know that he's not home, his back door is unlocked, and there's a baseball cap that could have belonged to Mr. Kirk. All supposition, so I won't be mentioning it and would prefer you didn't either."

"That's probably for the best, and I won't say a word to her," she promised, without including Gran. Trying to keep secrets from her was harder than frozen butter.

She did want to ask Ethan if they had any additional

leads on Smith and Chance but decided she might ask him that when Detective Jones wasn't nearby.

The man seemed to like her, but he clearly wasn't as happy to have her around when they were dealing with a case. He was only doing his job, but Maddie and Gran were Mavis's friends, and they couldn't let her deal with this by herself.

"I wonder if we might have a word with Mrs. Anderson alone?" Detective Jones addressed Gran and Maddie when they were back in Mavis's apartment.

"I'd like them to stay," Mavis said shakily.

Maddie's phone rang loudly in the small silence. It was Suzy and she was upset. Her parents were fighting and, not used to such a thing, she was panicking. Maddie promised to meet her at the gallery, aware that all ears in the room were listening.

"I'm sorry Mavis. Suzy needs my help with something."

"I'll stay here," Gran said firmly.

"Thank you, dear. Cora did sound very upset. I didn't realize Dan had such a temper until that day I saw him threatening Owen in the park."

The room was silent. Obviously, Mavis's hearing was better than average, and everyone else seemed to have grasped the short conversation. They were bound to take it out of context, and Maddie fervently wished she had taken the call outside.

"Are we talking domestic violence?" Detective Jones asked coolly.

"Of course not."

Jones stared at her for a moment. "Just in case, Sheriff, would you escort Ms. Flynn to the gallery, and I'll talk to Mrs. Anderson."

Ethan nodded and followed Maddie outside. "What's going on?" he asked.

She shrugged. "I don't know. There was a lot of yelling in the background, and Suzy's terribly upset. I don't believe they ever argue, so it's bound to seem worse than it is. I'm sure there's no need for you to come."

Ethan walked her to Honey "You heard the detective. And I have a couple of questions to ask Dan about what Mavis just said. I'll bring my own car and meet you there."

Maddie felt ill as she drove. One of her best friends was distraught, and a man she thought of as particularly sweet was perhaps not who she'd been led to believe.

Chapter Sixteen

Cora and Dan were in the small kitchen at the back of the gallery when Maddie and Ethan arrived. Suzy was outside, tears running down her face. She didn't seem fazed that Ethan was there, and she flung herself at Maddie.

"I can't believe this," Suzy sobbed. "All these years and hardly a cross word. I hate it," she wailed.

Maddie rubbed her back. "Shhh. It will be all right. Your parents love each other. This is just a blip. They'll get over it."

"I hope so, but they sound so mad at each other." Suzy sniffed.

"I'm just going inside to check on things," Ethan said.

Suzy's head jerked up. "Why is Ethan here?"

"Ah ..."

Maddie couldn't think quick enough, and Suzy lunged through the door of the gallery with Maddie on her heels.

Dan looked meaner than a bear woke from hibernation too early, and Cora was as pale as a meringue.

"So, you think I killed Owen Kirk?" Dan asked, hands on hips.

Suzy and her mother gasped.

Ethan put his hands up. "No one's saying that. But it seems you had words with him in the park. I'd just like to know what they were."

Dan studied his shoes for a moment, but when he looked up, he was even angrier. His voice was so cold that Maddie shivered.

"That man had no right to be hanging about here when my back was turned. He had no right to be talking to my wife every chance he could."

Cora gasped. "Dan, please tell me you didn't kill him?"

Dan seemed to shrink a little. "How can you ask me that?"

Cora's red-rimmed eyes welled up. "Up until a few months ago when you started behaving weirdly, I wouldn't have. And you just said ... You were jealous?"

Dan coughed. "I don't know about that, but it's not right for a man to hang around someone else's wife."

"So you said, but clearly something else happened between you and Owen?" Ethan pressed.

Dan gave the women an apologetic glance then shrugged. "I came to the gallery one afternoon to help Cora with a shipment. Owen was having a smoke by his van, but when he saw me, he hightailed it into the park looking as guilty as sin. He couldn't go far since, eventually, he'd need his vehicle. So, I followed him."

"And?"

Ethan's voice remained calm, but Maddie was worried for her friend's father.

Dan threw his arms out. "I told him to stay away from

Cora and not to park there again. Scared the life out of him," he said with no small amount of pride.

"You may like to think of a better choice of words, Dan." Ethan casually made a few notes in the small book he took from his breast pocket.

Dan shuffled his feet awkwardly. "Oh. Yeah. You know what I mean. He promised he'd move on, and he did. End of story."

"So, you never laid a hand on him? Or saw him at Sunny Days?"

"No. I did neither of those things. I was satisfied that he understood my message."

Cora was looking at Dan with concern. "Do you swear to it?"

He frowned. "I shouldn't have to, but I do. Why don't you believe me?"

"I want to, but you've been so secretive lately." Her face looked pinched, and she crossed her arms defensively.

"First I'm weird and now secretive?"

There was no way Dan could have looked more amazed.

Cora paled, but pushed on, her voice trailing away at the end. "Yes. You keep going away for hours, sometimes overnight. I wonder if you've met someone else."

Dan actually laughed. "Don't talk crazy. I have never so much as looked at another woman the way I look at you. Even if I wanted to, which I don't, I haven't got the energy for that kind of carrying on."

Cora looked a little mollified, but not satisfied. "So ... what do you do when you leave town?"

He glanced at Maddie and Ethan who were embarrassed to witness this frank conversation and stood awkwardly to one side.

"I can't believe you're asking this. You know I usually go watch a game. Any game," he ended on a note of desperation.

Cora frowned. "But why do you have to see so many? It's not like you don't have all the sports channels."

Dan sighed heavily. "The thing is, since I retired, I'm bored. This gives me a purpose. Something to fill my days."

She pursed her lips. "But you could help me here. I'm always asking, but you always find an excuse."

Dan took a step closer to his wife and gently took her hand. "Cora, as much as I like being with you, this gallery is your baby. I need something for myself, and I haven't found it yet."

Maddie felt like she and Ethan were intruding on a private moment and even more so when Cora hugged Dan.

"Then we need to find you that something. You should be as happy with your life as I am with mine. I do feel so much better, now I know you're not playing away from home."

Ethan and Dan snorted at the pun. Dan was a nut for sports, but Ethan loved them too.

"What about golf?" Maddie suggested.

Dan shook his head. "It's a pricey sport and the Country Club is a little la-de-da for me."

"We're hardly destitute. Play if it's what you want," Cora insisted.

"You can play some holes with some friends and then come back to the bakery or head to the diner instead of using the clubrooms," Suzy suggested.

"I guess I could give it a try," Dan said uncertainly, "until I find a small job to keep me occupied." Then he hugged Cora tighter.

They were adorable. He was so big and Cora so small

that Maddie had a lump in her throat. Beside her, Suzy was beaming.

"If you've asked all your questions, could we get going?" Maddie suggested to Ethan in a croaky voice.

He coughed. "Yes. Thanks for the honesty Dan."

But Dan and Cora only had eyes for each other, and Maddie grabbed Ethan's hand as they left.

He looked down at their entwined fingers. "Well, well. Seems romance is contagious."

She squeezed his hand. "I knew something was wrong between them, but I couldn't figure out what. Do you think Suzy knew they were having issues?"

"How would I know? You Girlz are a lot quicker on sensing these things than us mere males."

She snorted. "That's a bit sexist."

"Maybe. Tell me it's not true."

"It's entirely possible," she acknowledged. "And, I'm so happy that Dan had nothing to do with Owen's death."

"Me too. He's a great guy, and I believe him. Unless they're ridiculously good actors, what we witnessed couldn't have been more real. It just goes to show that couples need to be totally honest with each other."

"Like you and me?" she teased.

He nodded. "We're a work in progress."

"I like that. As long as we're progressing in the same direction."

"I don't think there's any doubt about that," he said firmly.

Chapter Seventeen

On Saturday the boys were back at the bakery and, this time, since Beth had to work in the salon all morning, and Layla was also working, they had another helper.

The sheriff was out of uniform but looking oh so handsome in jeans and a t-shirt. Maddie sat in the alcove where she did her accounts listening to the four of them. It was very entertaining, if somewhat distracting. Luke was attempting to keep them focused, but the twins were particularly boisterous this morning.

"Old people talk funny."

She poked her head around the corner to see that it was James speaking. Now she knew what to look for it was obvious that the cowlick would do very nicely in telling the boys apart.

Jesse wrinkled his nose. "Some of them smell funny too."

"Mothballs," Ethan explained.

The twins let out shrieks of laughter at the unfamiliar word, and Maddie pressed her lips together.

"They're white round globes, the size of a marble, and filled with a perfume type thing that stops moths from eating clothes and other material."

His technical description apparently needed a little work, since James was shocked.

"Moths eat clothes?"

"They do, which makes holes in them."

"Mom doesn't like it when we put holes in our clothes. Imagine if she saw a moth doing it?" Jesse flapped his arms and ran around James who made like he was trying to bite him.

Luke rapped on the counter with a spatula. "If these cookies are going to be done in time for the community center, we need to have more work and less talking."

"Sorry, Luke." Ethan grabbed the twins by the necks of their T-shirts and pulled them back into the production line. He picked up a spoon and began to drop dough on the tray.

Luke couldn't have been more surprised by Ethan's apology ... or the fact that he was actually making cookies.

"Ah, that's okay, Sheriff."

The boys were naturally not as formal with their uncle.

"Not that much dough Uncle Ethan! They have to be the same size. Use the ice cream scoop," James demanded.

"Is that what this is for?" He scooped cookie dough and squeezed it onto the baking tray. "Look at that. Who would have thought it had another great use?"

Maddie smiled at his amusement.

But there seemed to be another issue. The boys were whispering, and Jesse nudged James, who eyed Luke. "We think we need a different cookie."

Luke shook his head. "The two we're making will do for

this week. All the ingredients have been bought, and we know we have everything we need."

"But we're bored with these."

"You can't be bored with them, James. It's only the second time you've made them."

Both boys said something unintelligible.

Ethan laughed. "What they really mean is that they've eaten enough of this flavored cookie dough."

Luke issued a warning as he flattened the cookies. "The more you eat the less there is to sell."

"If we don't eat any more dough will you think about it?" Jesse tried a different tack.

Maddie went back to her accounts. The art of manipulation was strong in these two, and she heard the smile in Luke's voice.

"If you stop eating the dough, I'll speak to Maddie about another flavor for next time. Okay?"

There was the sound of single claps, and Maddie turned to see Ethan joining in some high fives. She had worked in one of the busiest family bakeries in New York City before Gran had manipulated her into coming home. Now, she couldn't imagine working anywhere else than Maple Lane Bakery. This was home, and the noise and fun was a reminder that family, annoying as they could be, was what made life interesting.

She finished what she was doing then walked around the huge counter to inspect the trays before Luke put them in the oven. They weren't as proportionally exact as her cookies and had a rustic quality, but she had no doubt they would taste as wonderful as last week.

"We're just about to bake them," James informed her.

"Good. As soon as they're done, we can take them to the community center."

Luke slid the trays in, then the four of them cleaned down the counter and tidied up the ingredients that hadn't been used while Maddie made up small boxes to save time later. Like last time, they would sell them singly to eat there or in boxes to take home.

Suzy had placed an order, as had Gran, Laura, and Angel.

"Why does that man always hang out at the center?" Jesse asked.

"What man?"

Ethan was instantly on alert, as was Maddie.

James was loading the dishwasher, unaware of their worry. "The one with the gray hair."

Maddie snorted, and the boys looked at her oddly, but Ethan shared a grin with her.

"Most of the people at the center on Saturday's have gray hair, and you've only sold cookies one time. You might like to be more specific."

James frowned. "We've seen him other times when we've gone to play basketball there. Before last Saturday. He didn't come inside any of those times and last week he didn't even buy our cookies. Mr. Clayton said we shouldn't worry about him, but he looked mean."

"Or sad." Jessie was helping Maddie with the boxes. His tongue poking between his teeth in concentration.

Ethan put his hand on James's shoulder and turned him around. He crouched down a little, so they were eye to eye. "Is this man from Maple Falls?"

He shrugged. "I've only seen him at the center."

"When we get to the center, can you point him out to me?"

"Sure. Is he a suspect?"

Ethan frowned. "A suspect for what?"

"Owen's murder."

Ethan shook his head. "We don't call it a murder unless we know for sure."

"But I heard you talking to Maddie about it the other day."

"Then you shouldn't eavesdrop. We don't know anything about this man, so we need to be careful. You know all about stranger awareness, don't you?"

He directed the question to both boys and they nodded.

"We study it in school," Jesse said.

"Great. He's probably a shy elderly man who's scared of kids and doesn't like cookies."

"Everyone likes cookies," James said emphatically.

"You'd think, but some people really don't."

The timer sounded, and Luke pulled the cookies from the oven. "These look good enough to eat."

"That's lucky," Ethan added and was treated to foul looks from the twins. "I never doubted for a second that they would be fantastic."

The boys didn't look convinced of his belated sincerity, but waited as patiently as was possible, until the cookies were cool enough before they packaged them.

"I'll drop the orders off later," Maddie said, as they loaded Honey with the boxes.

Ethan held her back when the boys went inside the bakery with Luke.

"Look who's across the road?" He pointed to where Laura and Rob stood closely.

"Laura's yoga would have finished some time ago. Have they been there all this time?"

"I think so."

She grinned. "They make a cute couple."

He pulled her close and dropped a kiss on the tip of her

nose. "Let's not say anything and give them a little time to come to their own conclusions about what kind of friends they are."

"From what I've seen, it's been a couple of months of avoidance from both sides."

"That's not long when you compare them to us."

"I guess not." Maddie was losing interest in the topic with Ethan's hands on her waist.

He pulled her to him and kissed her thoroughly before letting her go. His kisses were sweeter than any cake she'd ever made.

Chapter Eighteen

The community center was buzzing as was usual on a Saturday afternoon. A few different groups used the venue and sometimes the bookings overlapped. Currently, the cookie sale was happening in one half of the hall, while Noah Jackson's senior stretch group finished up on mats. Some of them would join the circle of the coffee or tea group, as it was affectionately known, when they were done.

There were plenty of interested looks from both groups when Maddie and the boys entered. But she imagined their interest was more for the sheriff who carried the majority of the boxes.

Gran made tea and coffee with Mavis's help while Maddie put a pile of cookie pieces on a plate to be used as samples. Unlike their weekday group this one was far more impromptu, but well supported thanks to so many people spreading the word about the boy's fundraising.

Mavis was the first one to buy a box. "These chocolate chip cookies are wonderful. You've done well, boys. And they're cheaper than Maddie's." She winked at her.

"I'm sure Maddie would have helped make them," Nora added.

She shook her head. "I honestly didn't. Like I said last week, this is all the work of the boys and Luke."

Nora made a rude sound of derision at the mention of Maddie's intern's name.

"He must find it difficult with people judging him by his brother's deeds," Mavis said. "His mom is such a sweetie. Luke must take after her."

Maddie knew Mavis thought she was being kind, but she wouldn't be the only one who heard the unspoken words that Luke's brother must have taken after his father. She also knew Mr. Chisholm was trying to atone for his part in his eldest son's criminal activity by cutting all ties with Mickey Findlay and his cohorts. This, in turn, had made Luke a lot happier and Maddie was pleased. He was still living with his parents, which would have been almost impossible if Mr. Chisholm hadn't admitted the error of his ways.

Just when the town was slowly coming to terms with what had happened last summer, now they had to deal with Owen's murder. It was bound to have a negative effect on morale, and it certainly didn't help that people like Nora were only too happy to remind everyone in case they did forget.

Maddie left them to help Mavis and Gran refresh cups, while the group munched on cookies and put orders in for whole boxes of them. She wondered what would happen when the boys had enough for their bikes. Maybe it would be a good opportunity for fundraising on a permanent basis for other causes in the community.

She was thinking on that when she saw the gray-haired man in the opposite corner of the room. He'd been there for some time ... not engaging with anyone. Every time Maddie looked up, he seemed to be looking at her. He looked familiar, yet she couldn't remember ever having met or spoken to him before.

His interest in her was a little unnerving, and she felt compelled to speak to him. She crossed the room. "Would you like to join the group for a cup of tea or coffee?"

A wariness had crept over his face as she'd approached. "Me? Why?"

She smiled gently, sorry that she had put him on the spot. "You looked lonely over here by yourself."

He looked down an elegant nose. "I can't imagine what would bring you to that conclusion."

He was very tall. His jumper frayed, with leather patches in the elbows that were cracked and what look liked paint on his fingers.

"You're not Nicholas Brack, are you?"

He paled. "How did you know that?"

"Lucky guess?"

His eyes narrowed and he shook his head.

She shrugged. "To be honest, I wasn't sure until I got closer. Until recently I didn't know you lived here. I saw a picture of you online."

He was more accepting of this and gave a wry smile.

"Sorry to disappoint you. That picture was taken more than a decade ago."

She smiled back. "It still looks like you. I could bring a coffee over here if you don't want to join in."

He nodded. "I admit, I'm not much of a mixer. I accept your offer. Black coffee, no sugar."

She went to the tray and poured his coffee. Gran and Luke were continuing to do the rounds, and the twins were delighting a small group with tales of their adventures. She brought him a cookie too.

"Here you go."

"How much do I owe you?"

"Nothing. It's a sample to entice you to buy more to support the boys or come to my bakery and buy other things." She winked.

He took a quick glance around the room, then smiled again. "I knew you were the owner of Maple Lane Bakery, even though I've never been inside it. Seems everyone knows who you are."

"It's a small town, but I bet you know all about that."

He grimaced. "Not small enough. Sorry, don't mind me. I'm not having a good day."

He didn't continue, but Maddie could tell he had something on his mind. "I'm sorry to hear that. Did you want to talk to me about something?"

He took a gulp of coffee and blanched as it burned his throat. "You're very astute."

"You've been looking at me for some time, and I don't think it was in the hopes of free coffee and cookies."

He looked around again. "I have been watching you and, as much as these cookies are great, you're right. You have a reputation for helping people sort out their troubles."

Maddie was so surprised by this she laughed aloud.

He frowned. "You can laugh, but it's true."

"Let me get this straight. You are in some kind of trouble ... and you want my help?" She was astounded. Here was a famous painter asking a baker to fix his troubles. It sounded more ridiculous said aloud.

He lowered his voice. "Big trouble, as it happens, and I have no idea what to do about it."

It was her turn to look around the room, but all she

could see were the usual crowd now that the stretching group had gone. Still, it didn't pay to be overheard.

"Do you want to talk here or go somewhere else?"

"You'd be willing to help me? Just like that?" he asked.

"Mr. Brack, I don't know you, but I'll help if I can. That's what we do in Maple Falls. Of course, it does depend on what the problem is. Have you done something illegal?"

His hand that held his cup shook, and he looked away. They'd been speaking quietly, and everyone else was at the other end of the room making plenty of noise. Still, she could sense his reluctance.

Eventually, he sighed. "It would be better to talk here. But I have to know if you could keep this between us—at least for a while?"

She said the only thing she could, because after all, famous or not, he really was a stranger to her. "Without knowing what it's about, I'm sorry, I can't promise."

He took a large breath. "Yes. It's illegal." He threw the words out as if they would choke him.

"I see. Will you tell me what it is?" She was glad he didn't want to go anywhere. In fact, now she knew it was illegal, having people close by made her feel a great deal safer. Not that he was the least bit threatening, but history had proved that you shouldn't be too quick to let your guard down.

He began to talk much more quietly, and Maddie had to step closer to hear him.

"The thing is, if I tell you what I know, then you'll be in as much danger as I am right now."

Maddie couldn't help taking another look around them. "Danger? From whom?"

He finished his coffee, the cookie, barely touched, lay in

a napkin, which he tucked into a pocket of his corduroy pants. "I believe you've met them."

She took a stab at guessing, since it seemed right. "The men from the gallery?"

"That's them. Scary lot, aren't they?" He tried to smile and failed miserably.

"Very," she agreed.

"I met Mr. Smith, first. He's the one with the charm. I was in a financial bind. Somehow, he knew. He offered me money. A great deal of it, actually. I wanted to refuse, but I was about to lose my house and, at the time, that felt like the worse thing in the world. My wife and I had lived there when we first married, before our careers took off. It has a lot of wonderful memories. Now I'm trapped into doing things I don't want to ... because I was a coward." His hands shook around the cup and his eyes looked haunted.

Maddie couldn't help her loud intake of breath. How was it possible that a painter of his ability could sink so low? She had to ask the elephant-in-the-room question. "I don't understand why you needed money, when your paintings sell for tens of thousands."

He flinched. "They did. To be honest, some still do. The problem is that I haven't been able to paint for some time, and once you've sold a painting, that's it. It's gone from you forever."

She chewed her lip. Perhaps it was like making and decorating a cake? You might spend hours on it and love the finished product but, ultimately, it was for someone else, and eventually ... you had to let it go. Of course, even the most expensive cake didn't bring in as much money as a highly prized piece of art.

"I don't mean to be indelicate, but what happened to all the money?"

He put one hand deep into his pocket and studied the floor. "Gambling. I'm not proud of it. In fact, I'm deeply ashamed."

She could see by his haunted look that this had been hard to admit. "What kind of gambling?" she probed gently.

"The bad, out of control, borrowing money kind. Like I say, I was about to lose my house."

"So, what did you have to do to earn the money?"

He shrugged. "Paint."

Maddie was totally confused. "You just said that you can't paint."

He toyed with the cup. Swirling the dregs, as if he were going to read tea leaves, which would have been difficult since he'd had coffee. His voice finally burst from him like a machine gun. "I can't paint anything new. I'm covering old paintings with new work."

"That painting of your wife's at the gallery, was it an original?"

"That's a copy. A good copy, but it's the last one I want to do. It's covering another painting that's superior to mine in every way."

"I don't understand. Why would you paint over a better painting with a copy of your wife's work? Surely someone would notice?"

"Someone like Cora Barnes? A lovely woman who only sees the good in people. A woman I went to school with. A woman I dated?"

Maddie held a hand to her throat. Suzy's mom and Nicholas Brack had been an item? How did Gran not know about that? This meeting was stretching her levels of credulity to the extreme.

He took a deep breath. "Nobody would understand that

it was the only way I could keep the few originals I had left and still pay my debts."

Sadness surrounded him and even though she knew he was wrong she couldn't stop a lump forming in the back of her throat.

"You need to talk to the sheriff," she managed to say.

He shook his head. "If I go anywhere near him or his deputies, one thing is sure, I'll only do it once."

"They've threatened you?"

"Many times. I had hoped that, after I painted over a couple, they would let me be. That I would have repaid their investment and more. It turned out to be wishful thinking. Once these people have their claws into you, there's no hope of escaping them."

He looked so depressed that Maddie couldn't help a measure of pity for him, despite his crimes.

"The only thing I can think of is tell Sheriff Tanner. I'll do it on the quiet. I promise, he'll be circumspect with who he tells."

Mr. Brack gave a heavy sigh. "I don't have anywhere else to turn, so I guess I'll trust you. It seems like I'm destined for jail or winding up like Owen."

"So, Owen was involved in this?"

"No, he wasn't. Not in the way you mean. Owen's estranged father, Bertram Langham, lives in Sunny Days retirement community. He's my friend. Or, was. I don't know if Bertram was coerced into handing me over or whether he was already in this foul business up to his neck. He had the connections with Smith and told him how desperate I was."

"So, Mr. Smith approached you?"

"He came to my house and offered me a way out. I had no idea he was a predator for people like me in general. He takes pleasure in it. He finds targets who are short of money then he offers to insure or help sell things for them. This is the reason he makes it his business to befriend people living in retirement communities ... so he can ascertain who's finding retirement tough."

"Isn't that helpful?" She was pretty sure she knew where this story was going.

"It sounds almost respectable, I grant you. Except for the fact that he would cream most of the money off the top, and the owners would get a fraction of the worth of something they might be genuinely fond of like an heirloom."

"That's not fair at all."

He nodded but held up a hand. "The bigger story, and where I fit in, is about the people who wouldn't sell and who caused him problems. Managing to wheedle himself inside their homes, he sneakily took photos, then brought them to me to recreate. Once he had the copy he would break in and swap it for the original."

"So you copied them and he sold the originals? Wouldn't that damage them?"

He nodded. "They're coated in a substance that allows the new coat to be wiped off using a special chemical that is safe."

"That's one heck of a scam. Surely they didn't all go through Mrs. Barnes's gallery?"

"Hardly any. I put my foot down about that, besides it was too close to home to be a safe way to do business."

"I'm so glad. Cora will be upset as it is. She thinks you're amazing."

"I'd hate for her to know. I'm still very fond of her, but I guess she will eventually. She's a wonderful woman, and I shouldn't have allowed them to use her at all."

"So, why have you decided to speak up now?"

"Mostly, it's Owen's death. He was a young man who did nothing wrong. He was just born to the wrong father."

She nodded, making a note to ask him about Bertram Langham later. "Mostly? What else?"

"The picture you found ..."

"Wait, you know about that?"

"Cora told me. She was upset that my painting had been damaged."

"Go on."

"Underneath what is actually a copy of my late wife's work, is a 'Sarah Mansell.'" He saw her confusion and gave a weak smile. "Sarah Mansell is an artist who, over the last decade, has sold each of her works for hundreds of thousands. She's sought after and the painting belonged to Nora Beatty, who had no idea of its worth. She bought it years ago before Sarah became famous."

"So, you've been helping them take money from people who can ill afford it?"

"I had to. Nora isn't a nice person, so I didn't feel bad about that, but I do feel bad for most of the others. What they could have gotten for their pieces could have set them up for life."

"Why do it then?"

"To be honest, it didn't take much to persuade me once I realized I could keep the last of my late wife's work and my home. My house has been in the family for generations, it would have been like losing a piece of myself." He looked down at his worn loafers, and his voice was barely audible. "Then again, I think I already have."

Maddie placed a hand on his arm, and he flinched.

"It was Bertram's idea to leave a couple of pictures at Cora's gallery as leverage in case Smith and Chance double-crossed us, which they seemed about to do. We were right to think so, but wrong to involve anyone else. It seems obvious now that when they disappeared from the stash Smith would force Bertram to tell him where they were."

"There are people who could have helped you."

"I don't know who. I got bigheaded and couldn't be bothered with the people I'd known from earlier days. I was insufferable and arrogant, and people only put up with that for so long."

Maddie hated to see a person so low, but right now, talking to Ethan was more important than making Nicholas Brack feel better. She hoped Ethan would be able to help because this was turning into chaos. A very dangerous chaos.

Chapter Nineteen

E than couldn't come by until that evening. He looked tired and Maddie told him to sit while she made him coffee and brought him a large slice of apple cake.

"Thanks, I need a pick me up, although seeing you has already lifted my spirits considerably."

She smiled, dropped a kiss on his lips, then took a seat opposite him at the large table. "Why did they need lifting?"

He shrugged. "Oh, the usual neighbor disputes along the county line—not to mention the murder. I wanted to come by last night, but it was very late by the time I got back."

"I'm happy for you to come by anytime, and I am glad to see you now. I have a lot to tell you."

He put the coffee cup down, giving the cake a wistful glance. "I can't leave you alone for five minutes, can I?"

Maddie stirred her apple and cranberry tea. "I'm pretty sure I'm not as alone as I'd like to think."

"What do you mean?"

"Detective Jones seems to have filled the gap your absences have created, and he wasn't even hiding it."

Ethan shrugged. "Most of the deputies were with me, so he offered to keep track of the Flynn women."

She was glad to hear that because she was worried—mostly for Gran, who knew Nicholas Brack and was also a regular visitor at the retirement community.

"Okay, but should he be so obvious?"

"When there's only one officer around, sometimes it pays to be obvious."

"That does make sense. Would you like something more substantial than cake to eat?"

"I thought you'd never offer."

She laughed and went to the walk-in chiller. "I have quiche or pasties?"

"Yes, please."

She poked her head out the door and saw his grin. "You want both?"

Ethan shrugged. "I think you know that's a rhetorical question."

She tutted as she warmed his food, then refreshed his coffee.

"Are you ready to tell all?"

"Eat first. You'll need your strength to hear this."

Ethan took her at her word and dug in. When he was ready for the cake, he slowed down to savor it.

It was time for the sad tale of Nicholas Brack, and it took a while to get through it.

Ethan ran a hand through his hair, having been silent the whole time, which was not like him. Usually he had a million questions. Now his hair stuck up at odd angles as he tried to condense everything.

"So, we have a man who loses his wife. Turns to

gambling and is on the cusp of losing all he owns. Smith allegedly contacts him and gives him a way to keep his house. Covering expensive paintings with other works which are then taken out of the country to be sold elsewhere?"

"That sounds right so far," she agreed.

"Where do Cora and the gallery fit in?"

"Nicholas was upset that Cora had been involved. He said only a few paintings went through the gallery. I do have a hunch though."

"Your hunches are often spot on. Tell me about this one." Ethan's tone was serious but there was still an affectionate twinkle in his eye.

She smiled at the way Ethan had slipped into sheriff mode. "I believe that there are two white vans."

He nodded. "You're absolutely right. Detective Jones is looking for it."

"Does he know whose it might be."

"He does, and you look like you do too."

"Bertram Langham's?"

"We don't know where it is, but Langham has a white van registered to him. He also has a garage adjacent to the apartments. The floor of that garage is covered in oil leaks."

"Wow, it's all coming together."

Ethan ran a hand through his hair. "I'd like to think so, but we are a long way from proving anything. If we could find Smith and Chance, we'd do a lot better."

"You've been warning me to be careful, Ethan. I hope you'll take your own advice. They are dangerous, and if they could kill Owen so easily, they won't hesitate to do so again."

He took her hands and held them between his. "I will

be careful, and you better stay away from the retirement community for now."

"Okay. Keeping Gran away will be harder."

He sighed. "It's like herding cats."

She laughed. "Cats are inquisitive."

"Not the word I was thinking of. Speaking of which, where is that monster of yours?"

"He's right beside you, under the table."

"He didn't whack me when I came in."

"You should take that as a compliment. It seems as if you've won him over."

"Since he owns a large portion of your heart, I'd better keep it that way." He kissed her palms then came around the table to kiss her thoroughly.

"That's better," she said with a grin.

He rubbed his thumb across her bottom lip. "I'd stay longer, but I need to stop by the station before I catch up with Detective Jones."

"A secret meeting?"

"No need to get excited. We have a catch up every day when there's a case on."

"Oh."

"Disappointed?"

"Not really. It's just a thing you do."

"Good point. See you tomorrow, Sherlock."

"Arrgh! Not you too?"

He laughed all the way to his car, and Maddie shut and locked the door with a smile. There was no point in worrying about Nicholas Brack tonight, and with Ethan and Detective Jones in town she felt safe.

"Come on, Big Red. Let's have an early night for a change."

Chapter Twenty

The next morning Jesse and James flew through the door of the shop. It banged against the jamb while the bell jangled maniacally. Maddie dropped a tea tray on the table in fright, thankfully not breaking anything and grateful that the cup and pot were empty.

"Whoa, you two. Where's the fire?"

They screeched to a halt, giving Maddie the time needed to figure out who was who.

"I didn't see a fire." Jesse looked at her like she was crazy.

"I meant, why are you in such a hurry?"

"We just met a man who wants to buy a whole batch of cookies. Do you think he means a tray? Anyway, he wants them before we go to the community center this weekend. He wants to get some before the others."

Nora Beatty was sitting at the table by the window, giving the boys a disapproving look, so Maddie pushed the wriggling boys into seats at another table.

"Inside voices, please, guys." She sat beside them. "Who is this person, and how do you know him?"

"We don't know him. He's a stranger." James said.

"Should you be talking to a stranger?"

Their faces reddened.

"But he wants a heap of cookies." Jesse grumbled.

"I think that's the point. You know nothing about this man and yet he knows about your cookies."

"So, it's a no?" James pouted.

"Look, I know you have your hearts set on the bikes, and you're doing a great job with raising money for them, but slow and steady is preferable to risking your safety."

"He seemed nice," Jesse said sullenly.

"Okay. I get it. You're annoyed, but I'm not as happy as you about this, so give me some details."

James sensed capitulation. "Like what?"

"What did the man look like? How does he know about your cookies? Where does he want to collect them from?"

"He said it was a surprise for his friend and he'd contact us before Saturday to get them. We're only telling you because we have to use your kitchen and your ingredients to make them." James looked like he wished he hadn't mentioned it at all.

Maddie went cold. Telling a child that they couldn't tell anyone about a meeting rang all her alarm bells. "You haven't said what he looked like."

Jesse frowned. "He was really big and he had dark hair. He was wearing a suit and a big coat, which is funny because it's warm outside."

For the sake of the boys Maddie swallowed the fear that the image of Chance brought on.

"I want you two to promise me that you won't meet with this man, no matter how much he offers to pay you."

Reluctantly they did.

"I'm going to trust you while I find out about this man.

If he's okay then we can make more cookies for him, but he will need to come here and collect them from me or pick them up from the community center. Okay?"

Hope spread across their less than clean faces.

"You're the best, Maddie," James said.

Nora made a rude sound, making Maddie think that she had heard every word.

"Thanks guys, and I'm so glad you told me. You can have a cookie to take to school for listening so well."

They shot over to the display case where Laura was loading a tray with peanut butter cookies. The choice was quick and easy.

Maddie put one each in separate paper bags. "Off you go and no talking to strangers." She saw them out then turned to her customer. "Do you need anything else, Mrs. Beatty?"

"You can top up this teapot with hot water," she said gruffly.

"Certainly."

Nora had placed a notebook on the table beside her cup and she rubbed her hand over the worn cover. "You did the right thing there."

"Sorry?"

"What you said to those boys. They shouldn't be talking to strangers."

Maddie couldn't believe Nora was on her side. "I agree."

"There are a few in town right now."

Prickles raced along her skin. "Strangers? Can you tell me about them?"

Nora shook her head. "I could, but I wouldn't like to get in trouble."

"It might help with the investigation into Owen's death."

Nora pursed her lips, something she did so often that her lips had formed permanent small lines around the outside. "How come you want to involve yourself in that business. You have everything going for you, unlike others."

Maddie was surprised by the jealousy she heard in Nora's words.

"I do feel very lucky, but I work hard to achieve it. I love Maple Falls. It hurts us all when something ugly happens to one of us."

"Owen Kirk wasn't one of us," Nora stated, flatly.

"He was a nice person."

"A nice person wouldn't hang around retirement communities or galleries for hours, without talking to people, would he?"

"You know about that?"

"Everyone knows about him parked up at the retirement community. Mavis made sure of it. She likes to feel important, that one."

"And the gallery?"

"I saw it with my own eyes. I walk the town every day for exercise and there he was, most mornings in the alley way, just sitting in his delivery van. Watching everyone."

"I wonder why?"

"You should ask Bertram Langham. He's another dodgy one. Always in and out of everyone's apartment asking questions."

"I believe he has been brought to the attention of the Sheriff. What about the other strangers?"

"Scary lot, they are. Slinking around in the shadows. Making poor Nicholas worry. I hope you and the Sheriff get them out of town real soon."

"Can you tell me what they look like?"

"The boys did a good enough job of that. Now, where's my water?"

Maddie blinked a couple of times. The connection with Nicholas Brack was very interesting. He was definitely involved in the paintings, but Nora was confirming more than that. Their conversation was clearly done, so she picked up Nora's teapot and went to refill it.

When her customer was served and had turned her back, Maddie went to call Ethan from upstairs. Big Red followed her and pushed between her and the table so he could sit on her lap. He looked at the phone as she dialed as if he was interested in the call.

"What do you think? Are things are going to fall into place now."

He rubbed his head under her chin and purred.

"I'll take that as a positive sign."

When Ethan didn't pick up she left a message, but before she could go downstairs Gran joined her in the apartment and sat opposite her at the table.

"I just saw Nora leave. She made a snide comment about you and the Girlz interfering in police business. Something's up and I want to know what, young lady."

Maddie sighed and explained what she could.

"So we really have ourselves a big fat mystery?" Gran leaned in to give Big Red a scratch between his ears.

"It already was a mystery as soon as Owen was found with no clear reason for his death. Then there's the whole painting thing."

Gran nodded sadly. "I guess I was hoping it wouldn't escalate the way it has."

"I hear you, but I feel that we've only just touched the

tip of the iceberg. So many things have happened and yet a cohesive link is eluding me."

"What does Ethan say?"

"I'm still waiting to hear from him. He'll be really worried about the boys and I imagine Layla will be furious about it too."

Big Red growled at Maddie's fingers as they tapped his back. She returned to the soothing pats he preferred.

Gran nodded. "As a mother, this will be a shock. Grown men coercing children into meeting secretly ..." She made a rude noise.

"Exactly. The hardest thing is that Ethan will need to catch these guys in the act of doing something, otherwise it's all hearsay and conjecture."

"The law can be a tricky beast." Gran frowned.

"It can be, that's for sure." Maddie agreed. Everyone was frustrated it seemed.

Gran looked to the stairway and lowered her voice. "I wonder if Laura is going to spend time with Deputy Jacobs."

Maddie's eyebrows rose. "Wait. Where did that come from?"

"Seriously? Those two have been flirting with each other since the animals were found. He goes red in the face every time he sees her and she's doing her best to avoid him. Classic shy people attitude when they're interested but scared to do anything about it."

"Gran, you old devil. I had a feeling you were up to your matchmaking tricks again."

Gran sniffed. "I don't know what you mean."

Maddie laughed. It was a relief to talk about something else with a lighter mood. Maybe this was another of Gran's plans. "Sure, you do."

"All I'm saying is that they need a small push. Speaking of which . . ."

A knock on the stairwell heralded Ethan's arrival.

"That was quick," she said to him while giving Gran a warning look.

She returned an innocent one

"Sorry, did I interrupt something?" he hesitated at the doorway, hat in his hand.

"Nothing that won't keep," Maddie said.

Gran waved his worries away. "I'm just going. I have a meeting at the community center."

"Be careful," Maddie and Ethan said together.

Gran gave them a knowing smile. "I will. Jed's taking me and bringing me home, so don't worry. With a minder like him, I'll be right as rain."

Ethan waited until she had reached the last step. "She knows?"

"Everything. Sorry, but Gran has a sixth sense when it comes to sniffing out something cooking and she has so many friends who want to update her that having reciprocal information really works."

He laughed. "Sounds like someone else I know."

Maddie shrugged, unable to deny it and surprised she hadn't thought of this connection already.

"Is that why you let me tag along?" she asked sweetly.

"Let you? That's an interesting way of putting it. Seems to me that I don't have much of a say in whether you 'tag' along or not most times."

Maddie shrugged. "I can't help it if people want to tell me things when you're not around, so I have to follow them up."

"Really? You and Gran have the town eating out of your

palms. Almost literally. They feel a closer connection with both of you than I can ever hope to emulate."

"I think you'll find that the female population would be only too happy to be interrogated by our handsome Sheriff."

His cheeks pinked up and he waved this away. "Pure fabrication on your part."

"Does Deputy Jacobs have a girlfriend?"

His eyebrows shot up so high they touched the wavy lock of hair he tried to slick back.

"Good grief how does that even come up in this conversation?"

"Just something I heard about him liking a certain woman, not too far from us."

"You mean, Laura?"

It was her turn to be surprised. "You think it's true?"

"He's been talking non-stop about her baking. They see each other in the park every Saturday, and sometimes walk his puppies together."

"He does yoga?" she asked.

"I guess it's a new thing," he smirked.

"Well, well. Laura hasn't said a word about it."

He shrugged. "Makes a change for someone to keep things to themselves around here. Although, I am surprised that Gran hasn't picked up on it."

"She did, but Laura won't acknowledge it."

"And we know what that means. You'll be looking for something that might or might not come to fruition and wanting to help it along. No wonder she hasn't mentioned it."

She shook her head. "Not me. I think a couple has to move at their own pace. There's no hurry, is there?"

"A couple like us?" He moved closer and pulled her to

her feet so that they stood toe to toe, forcing Big Red to jump to the floor.

She nodded, liking the way his breath touched her face as he bent towards her. Liking his arms around her. Liking the way he kissed her gently.

He leaned back a little. "We might have plenty of time, but I'm not as patient as you."

"You think I'm patient?" She wrapped her fingers in his dark hair and pulled his head down to hers once more.

They kissed as if they wouldn't let go and when it ended they were both short of breath.

Maddie gazed into his usually calm blue eyes. They seemed to spark as if an inner heat was trying to escape. The fireworks she'd just experienced reflected how she felt about him. How she thought about him every day.

"Owww!"

Big Red had nipped Ethan's ankle. Now he curled around Maddie's legs as if to say she should step away from the Sheriff.

"You stop that. Ethan is our friend and he can kiss me anytime he likes."

Big Red growled and slunk off to the couch, where he settled himself while continuing to glare at Ethan.

"Sorry about that."

"You might be. He looks anything but sorry."

"He is very protective of me and is usually fond of you. I guess he'd be fine if you don't actually touch me," she teased.

He shook his head. "That's helpful."

"Hopefully the more I see you the quicker he'll get over his jealousy."

"Then I'd better stop by more often." He grinned.

"Now what was so important about the boys and their cookies?"

Maddie had been dreading this, but she took a deep breath and explained that the twins had been approached and what she had said. Ethan's face went dark and his eyes flashed dangerously.

"I'd better get to Layla's and tell her."

She was sorry to see him go, but understood completely. "Please don't be mad at the boys. I think they now understand how dangerous meeting strangers away from friends and family can be. I'd hate for them to have to give up on their cookie making because of those crooks."

"Rest assured, if they don't understand, they will do by the time Layla has finished with them. I'm not sure if Layla will allow them to continue, but hopefully we can work something out. They'll need close supervision until this mystery is solved. I'll see you tomorrow."

Ethan was on a mission. No one could potentially hurt his family and get away with it. She knew he would follow the law, but she didn't envy Smith and Chance when the sheriff got hold of them.

When he'd gone she sat on the couch beside Big Red, wanting a cuddle. He turned away from her.

"Fine. Be like that. I've got work to do anyway."

If a cat could blow raspberries, that's the sound Big Red made as she went down the stairs.

Chapter Twenty-One

That Tuesday, Maddie arrived at the community center with her containers of cookies and cakes as usual. She glanced around the room. Gran and Mavis were busy making the tea and coffee, so Maddie put out the food before checking the room again.

Nicholas Brack had arrived and stood to the back of the room once more. He nodded to her and she finished serving Nora Beatty, who gave her a close look.

Maddie smiled and went to pour a coffee. Then she took a cookie in a napkin and went over to him.

"Here you go," she said in a normal voice.

He handed her five dollars.

"It's happening tonight." He spoke just above a whisper.

Maddie noticed that he had a bruised eye. "What's happening tonight?"

"The final load of paintings is being taken out of town."

"Not via the Gallery?"

His eyebrows lifted. "There was no way they would use Cora again after the little stunt you pulled."

"Did they do that to you?" She pointed to his face.

"It's nothing. In fact, I count my blessings it wasn't worse. It's my saving grace and my curse that they need me for a while longer. After this I'm not so sure they'll feel the same way."

"Hopefully we can circumvent that, but aren't you afraid that Smith or Chance will be here today?"

"You can take the credit for them most certainly not being here."

"How so?"

"You thwarted their plan to buy cookies from the boys. They had intended to bribe their way into the last of the apartments in the retirement community using the boys and their cookies as bait."

"No! Using children that way is shameful."

Nicholas gave a small smile. "To most, that would apply. You saw what happened to Owen Kirk. With these men, anything goes, and shame isn't part of their repertoire. They've had to think up another plan, which is why they're elsewhere. Now, what do you intend to do about the paintings?"

"Are you sure you want to be involved?"

"I'm deeply involved already. I want to make amends before it's too late."

"I appreciate it as will all of Maple Falls."

"I don't think they'll be quite as forgiving to the con-man I've become."

She put a hand on his arm. "You underestimate this town."

"For my sake, I hope so. I lived here for many years when I was younger, and I was a pompous fool back then. Ask your Gran. Then again, I probably still am."

A shadow passed by the door. Maddie and Nicholas tried to see who it was, but the person was gone.

"I think we've been seen together enough already. I'll take a box of cookies to make it seem legitimate for me to be here."

Maddie nonchalantly collected one of the last boxes, aware that Gran and Nora were keeping their eyes on her, and handed it to him.

Nicholas passed her more money. "I look forward to these and your help."

There was little hope in his voice. Then he slipped out the back door without turning around. Maddie hoped he would come out of this okay.

It was hard to concentrate on anything, especially when she heard Mavis say that Bertram Langham had not returned yet, and she thought she might be stuck with Rembrandt. The poor woman was a bundle of nerves and had apparently been hounding Gran all morning for reassurance that she was safe in her apartment. She was frustrated that there wasn't more security at the retirement community and shocked that anything bad was happening there.

She helped as usual with the clean-up, but her continued comments set Maddie's teeth on edge. Naturally, she felt very sorry for her. She no longer could trust that she was living in a safe community due to the missing man and the odd noises next door. No amount of words appeared to soothe her, and Maddie was more worried about Nicholas right now.

As she was leaving, Maddie saw Detective Jones in his car across the road. Not that she could actually see him, but his jet-black sedan was rather obvious these days. Which seemed odd. He was too clever to be seen if he didn't want to be, so was it intentional?

Should she go speak to him or would that blow his

cover? She might have helped Ethan a couple of times with his cases, but she was very much a novice in the ways of detectives and their methods.

She desperately needed to talk to Ethan about Nicholas. This case seemed like it was headed towards a climax with the paintings leaving tonight, even though she had no idea how that would look.

Ethan had plans to stop by tonight, something he was making a habit of lately, which was fine by her. In fact, she looked forward to the chance to talk privately, something that wasn't always easy to achieve at the bakery ... or anywhere around Maple Falls, really. As the sheriff, Ethan was always on duty even if he was officially off. People had no issue with stopping him anytime of the day to chat or have a moan. Maddie was grateful that when she shut the bakery door she was off limits except by phone.

Maddie drove Honey home, and when she was safely in the garage, called Ethan from the car. It went to voicemail. She left an urgent message for him to call her, but that wouldn't do.

She ran inside, checked that Luke and Laura were okay and ran upstairs to call Deputy Jacobs on the private number he had left with her when he had taken the unclaimed puppies home last summer. To her relief he answered and wasn't far away. He promised to stop by very soon.

She went downstairs to find that Jed had dropped Gran off, and she had plenty of questions. Maddie had hoped to have some privacy with Rob by taking him upstairs, but that didn't look likely.

"I thought I'd stop by and tell you that the community group are loving the cookies and they even have some outside orders for next week. At this rate the boys should be able to get their bikes fairly soon."

"That is good news."

Gran was watching her closely. "What did Nicholas Brack want with you today? I saw him buy cookies, but I'm guessing that wasn't his reason for being there?"

Before she could answer, Rob bounded up the path and received a swipe across his ankle as he came inside the open door. He jumped in fright and Laura raced to his aid.

"Are you okay, Deputy Jacobs? You're such a naughty boy!"

He frowned. "Pardon me?"

She flushed. "I was talking to Big Red."

"Ah, of course." He grinned. "He didn't hurt me. I guess he was making sure I knew he was here."

"Maybe he smelled the puppies on you?"

"That could be it," he said, graciously.

Big Red was a tyrant until he got used to a person. Even now, after being told off by Laura he was pressed up to her legs as if he was saying sorry for upsetting her.

Rob dragged his attention away from Laura—whose pink cheeks only enhanced her natural beauty—to ask, "What was it you needed to talk to me about?"

Maddie could feel Gran's and Laura's interest pique. There was no way to pretend that it was nothing, and she trusted everyone in the room. So, with Luke in charge of the shop she took them upstairs and told them about Nicholas Brack.

"I know he's up to his eyeballs in this, but he really is trying to make amends. He's been scared of Mr. Smith and Mr. Chance for a long time."

"I can't believe he could deceive all those poor residents. It's not like they're rich." Gran was understandably angry at the hurt this was causing her friends.

"I'm going to call Detective Jones to help me with this until I can get ahold of Ethan."

"He was outside the community center this morning," Maddie told Rob.

"Detective Jones? Doing what?"

"Sitting in his car."

"That's odd." He seemed to remember that this wasn't prudent to say, and he walked to the door. "Please excuse me, I'll call him now."

He went outside to make the call, and Gran welcomed the chance to inject her own thoughts and questions.

"Why did Nicholas tell you and get you involved in this?"

"He knows how much we care about the community. I think he's tired of being scared and saw an opportunity to unburden himself. He's also sorry for what he's done."

"In that case, I'm glad he's trying to make amends before anyone else gets hurt or ripped off."

"Did those men you mentioned kill Owen?" Laura was pale.

"I think they might have. Although no one's ready to say if the two are connected or not."

"Ask Rob, Laura," Gran insisted.

"Me? Why would he tell me?" Her voice came out in a squeak.

Gran slapped her thigh. "You are funny. He'd tell you anything because that man can't take his eyes off you."

"Don't be ..." Laura spluttered, unable to actually tell Gran off.

"Silly? You can say it, but we all know, that's the one thing I'm not. When will you Girlz take matters into your own hands? Men have to ponder things for a bit, like getting the temperature just right for a cake, but you can always put the heat up a little to speed up the process. If you care to."

Sharing a house together had obviously opened some lines of communication which Maddie had not been privy to, which Laura was potentially regretting, and which Gran was not done with.

"He likes you and you like him. At least ask him out for tea. Although, he's probably the coffee type of man."

Laura sat down with a thump at the table, the fight leaving her. "He does prefer coffee, but that's all I know about him."

Gran sat down beside her and patted her hand. "You know he loves animals, he's single, and has a good job."

"He's also very nice," Maddie felt bound to add.

Big Red took the chair on her other side and butted his head against her arm. Laura could only resist so long then she raised her hand in surrender.

"Okay, stop this before Rob comes back and hears you."

"What might I hear?"

Laura swung towards the door so fast she almost fell off her chair. Rob rushed to her side to make sure the chair didn't topple, then he leaned down and put an arm around her shoulders, his face etched with concern.

"Are you okay, Laura."

"Thank you. I'm fine. Really." She looked pointedly at his arm.

He put it behind his back with an awkward smile and stood. "Do you have more information to add?"

She shook her head. "It's nothing to do with the case."

"Okay." He didn't appear to believe her, but didn't push. "Detective Jones is on his way."

"We'll leave you to deal with that." Gran led the way out, and Laura reluctantly followed.

For someone who professed not to be interested in the Deputy, she shared a smile with him until Gran stopped on the step.

"Laura's keen to do some dog walking if you need someone to help with the puppies."

He frowned. "I can't say I do. I enjoy getting out with the rascals."

Rob had rescued two white Shih Tzu puppies when no one claimed them last summer. They were possibly related, ridiculously cute, and he was as besotted with them as Maddie and Gran thought he was with Laura.

"See, Gran." Laura's mouth turned down.

Gran gave Rob a particularly firm look and after looking backwards and forwards between the two of them, he finally got the point.

"But if you have the time, you could come with us? We take long walks around the lake every Sunday morning and during the week sometimes."

Laura didn't know how to respond, but that didn't stop Gran.

"She'd love to. Give her a call later, and you can work out a time. Come on Laura. We have some things to attend to. I'll be ready when you come to pick me up," she said to Maddie.

Shell-shocked, Laura followed meekly, and when she stopped at the gate to look back at the bakery, Rob stood at the door looking bemused. He waved. It looked odd from a man in uniform and Maddie struggled not to laugh.

"Your grandmother is a force to be reckoned with."

"I know, and I'm sorry if she badgered you into that."

"Not at all, but I do worry that Laura is perhaps not as eager as Gran made out?"

"I can't speak for Laura, apart from saying that she does love animals, including Big Red."

The cat in question lifted his head from where he lay under the hedge having followed Gran and Laura out.

Rob laughed. "He's still the biggest cat I've ever seen, and has the personality to match."

Maddie approved of his comment which was factually correct, just as she approved of Gran's matchmaking. Not that she would admit it to her. The last thing they needed was to encourage Gran in her other not-so-secret life's work.

Rob's phone beeped. "Detective Jones wants to meet me at the station instead."

"Do I need to come?"

"I shouldn't think so, unless you have something else to add?"

"No. I've told you everything. I'm going to clean up then visit Mavis at the retirement village. She's been worried about what happened to Owen, and I promised Gran we'd visit and check on her apartment, so she feels safer. Ethan asked us to stay away but Mavis was still upset when she went home after the group meeting this afternoon."

"I guess if the detective has moved on it must be safe. Hopefully, he has good news."

He had a spring in his step as he left, and she didn't think it could be attributed to her contribution to the case or any good news concerning it.

Luke, who had been standing in the doorway of the shop as often as he could, came out to see if she was okay.

"That was intense," he said.

"It was. I hate to ask, but could you close up tonight? I

was going to take Gran to see Mavis around supper time, but I think I'd rather go when it's still light, and Laura just got dragged home by Gran."

He laughed. "I heard. Poor Laura. She'll be all jittery now she has a kind of date with Deputy Jacobs. No problem with closing up. There are only a few customers, and I've begun the cleaning."

Again, Maddie marveled at Luke's astuteness. Not many young men would respond the way he did to the dramas of the Girlz. "Whatever would I do without you?"

"I hope you never have to find out." He grinned.

"Trust me, your job security is not threatened."

They laughed again as Luke emptied the dishwasher and Maddie automatically got a few things ready for tomorrow, all the while hoping that she and Gran could appease Mavis.

Chapter Twenty-Two

Before she headed out to pick up Gran, Maddie got an odd call. When she picked up, someone was there, she heard breathing.

"Hello?" she said several times.

No one answered. Then the call was cut off. She redialed the number, and it went straight to voicemail. A terse message from Nora Beatty told Maddie she was busy and might get back to her if she left a number. With emphasis on the 'might'.

Maddie barely managed a goodbye to Luke as she raced out the door. She beeped the horn outside Gran's, something she would never normally consider. This was evidently cause for alarm as Gran came out with her bag and a floral apron still tied at her waist. Laura stood at the door wringing her hands, and Gran barely got her seat belt done up before Maddie swung Honey back down Plum Place.

"Slow down, dear. I know you have more news, but we do want to arrive in one piece."

Maddie had thought about going on her own, but Gran

would have been furious. She told her about the call. "I tried Ethan again with no luck." She thrust her phone at Gran. "Please keep trying, and if you can't get him, Rob's number is there too."

Minutes later they drove into the retirement community and parked close to Nora's apartment, which was at the end of the block where Mavis lived.

"You wait here. I'll wave to you if everything's okay."

Gran nodded, not looking overly impressed with the request. "I'll keep trying these numbers, but don't you go anywhere that doesn't look safe."

Maddie ran to Nora's apartment and knocked at the door. There was no answer and her pulse spiked. Surely Nora wasn't in the sights of the forgers? Next, she tried Mavis's apartment, and was reassured to see her safe and well.

"Hello dear, what are you doing here now? I thought you were bringing dinner?"

"We were, but I got a call from Nora, so I thought I'd pop in to see her first. She doesn't appear to be home. Any idea where she might be?"

"Hmmm, let me see. I think she was going to Destiny this afternoon to see her sister. Bernie was driving her. He had a few errands and was happy to bring her home. Strange that she would call you to stop by if she wasn't going to be home."

Maddie breathed a sigh of relief. "That's okay then. I must have misunderstood."

"You're very pale. Do you want to have a seat until you feel better?"

She had opened the door wider, and Maddie could see a man sitting on the edge of a sofa. He turned, and his hooded eyes bore a hole through her. Mr. Smith. Mavis had no idea she had let a murderer into her home. A murderer who didn't seem too surprised to see Maddie.

"I wouldn't like to interrupt anything."

"Nonsense. This is Mr. Smith. He's from the insurance people and came to look at some of my paintings. I told him they weren't important ones, but he's been doing the rounds of the entire community this week. I was busy with the community center work, so I guess I might be last."

"We've met," Maddie said coolly. "Which insurance company do you represent?" she asked, as she followed Mavis into the compact sitting room.

"Mine of course. Agreeable Insurance." Mavis answered for him.

His smile was that of a crocodile about to dine on an unsuspecting bird, but Maddie knew his character, even if she didn't know his real name. Mavis and people like her were sitting ducks for the unscrupulous.

"I was under the impression that you were an art connoisseur?"

His smile tightened. "A man can be more than one thing, Ms. Flynn."

She nodded. "That's true. Just like a woman can. I hope you're able to assure Mrs. Anderson that her paintings will be safe?"

He managed an air of nonchalance. "That's what I do. Just in case something happens to the art we like to make sure the insurance policy is enough to cover them."

"So, you offer this service to other retirement communities?"

"Naturally. Perhaps you or your Gran have some works you'd like an assessment of? I could go by the cottage or the bakery anytime."

A chill went up her spine. He knew who she was and

where she lived. It was naïve to think he wouldn't have found out about her after the gallery incident. She couldn't prove it, but this was definitely a warning to back off, or else.

"Oh, I believe we're well taken care of, thanks. Gran and I own nothing of value."

He raised an eyebrow and stood. "I guess it depends on what's the most important thing to you. Thank you, Mrs. Anderson, for your hospitality. I'll be in touch soon. Now I better visit my other clients before it gets too late."

Maddie heard his threat but tried not to show how frightened she was. Mavis became a little giddy as she saw him out. Maddie watched from the hall to make sure he actually left. When Mavis came back, she dropped into her chair.

"Isn't he just the loveliest man?"

Maddie counted to ten under her breath. "I don't care much for insurance people."

"I understand, but he really cares. Bertram has been talking about him for some time, but I kept putting him off. Then out of the blue, he turned up when I got back from the community center. I guess it was meant to be."

Maddie was absolutely sure it wasn't. "Did he take any art?"

"Not yet. He looked around first then picked my grand-mother's portrait as one he'd like to get valued."

"That's good. Mavis, Gran is out in the car. I'll just go get her. I'll be back soon."

"Why would you leave her there? Did you think I might not be home yet? I'll go ahead and make fresh tea for her."

Maddie let her answer her own questions and opened the door. Smith had disappeared and there wasn't anyone around, but her skin still prickled. This place was not safe for any of them. Not until Ethan, Rob, or the detective arrived. Why weren't they here by now? She could see Gran in the car on the phone and saw her shake her head.

"Mavis?"

"Yes, dear?"

"Gran thought you might like to have supper at the cottage instead."

Mavis came out to the doorway. "Gran's still in the car?"

"Yes, she's waiting for us."

"I don't understand. I was making tea?"

"I know, but wouldn't this be more fun?" Maddie used all her charm to entice her.

Her round face lit up. "Yes, it would. We can all have a good gossip over some of Gran's amazing cooking. Let me get my bag and feed Rembrandt."

Mavis could not be hurried, and after ensuring that the apartment was locked up three times, Maddie eventually got her into Honey. As she drove, she gave a thought to Nora. If she really was with Bernie, she had to be safe, didn't she?

When they got to Gran's, Maddie walked them to the door.

"You go in and make yourself comfortable, Mavis. Laura's there, somewhere." Gran shooed her down the hall then turned to Maddie with a sigh. "You're not coming in?"

"No. I can't. I have to find someone to make sure the rest of the residents of the retirement community are protected. After what Nicholas Brack said, I have a bad feeling several people there are in danger. People who could point the finger at forgers and murderers."

Gran hugged her. "When I saw that man come out of Mavis's place, I felt sick. I knew from your description who he was, and I hunkered down as he walked away. I couldn't see exactly where he went, but he headed back towards the main entrance."

"He also threatened us—you and me in particular, but he might have meant Angel, Laura and Suzy too. Please keep Mavis and Laura here, and make sure this place is locked up tighter than a bank."

"I certainly will. And you make sure you don't do anything to get yourself hurt."

They hugged again, then Maddie hurried to Honey and made her way back to the retirement community. She drove slowly around small roads between the apartments and was about to leave again when she spied the detective. He was outside Bertram Langham's back door looking out over the fields. He turned to face her, but she was too far away to see his features. Finding a parking spot around the corner, she ran back to him.

"Did you hear about Nicholas Brack?" she asked breathlessly.

Detective Jones frowned. "Obviously you have. We have him at the station in protective custody. Sheriff Tanner brought him in."

"Thank goodness. Smith was here not long ago. I can't reach Ethan or Rob." Then she explained what had happened.

"Ms. Flynn, I was assured by the sheriff that you would stay away from there. We have Smith and Chance under surveillance. They won't be getting away, but you could have been hurt, and you may have already compromised this investigation."

"I couldn't ignore that phone call or Mavis's plea," she said helplessly.

"Don't you think that's exactly what their plan was? To get you here?"

Maddie was at a loss for words. She hadn't thought of that—the fact that Gran might have been hurt along with Mavis because she couldn't leave things alone.

"I suggest you head on home now and leave this to the professionals, but I thank you for your help so far and for being so community minded."

The brush off was complete. Maddie headed back to Honey feeling like a willful child, which didn't stop her being worried about everyone. Where was Ethan? Maddie hoped he was safe. For him not to return any calls, he must be neck deep in the case somewhere. At least she had been able to pass on the information to Detective Jones who was heading the case since Owen's murder; maybe some of it had been news to him. And Nicholas Brack was safe, which made her feel a little better.

She hadn't gotten back to Honey when a shout halted her steps. She turned, knowing where it had come from, and ran back to where she had left Jones. A man was dragging the prone detective towards the pond at the bottom of the garden. In a panic she searched for a weapon. She should have paid more attention to who else was near.

Too late! A hand grabbed her from behind.

Chapter Twenty-Three

Mr. Smith turned her around to sneer into her face, a little spittle captured in the corner of his mouth.

"I knew you'd be trouble, but I underestimated just how much."

He shook her until her teeth rattled, which also prevented her from screaming. Then he put a hand across her mouth. He might be smaller than Chance, but his fingers were like iron. She twisted and tried to bite him, but nothing she did had any effect.

A deep voice boomed. "Let's go. We can't do anything about her here. Not with her boyfriend on the loose."

She already knew that Chance was fast, and he was now beside them. He also looked meaner than his boss who nodded in the direction of Jones's body where it lay near the pond.

"What about the detective?" Smith asked.

"He'll be fine. The way I hit him ... he's not coming around from that any time soon. If at all. Lucky you saw the baker come back before she could alert anyone. Not that anyone around here seems to pay any attention to what's going on."

Maddie hoped that wasn't true, especially right now.

Chance picked her up under one arm like a doll, his other hand replacing Smith's on her mouth and jogged to their car, probably the same one they'd used before but with different plates. It was hidden behind a large tree which was why she hadn't noticed it.

Smith opened the back door and Chance threw her in. The breath was knocked from her body as she hit the opposite door, and she could only wheeze her indignation at his treatment. She had to scoot along or get squashed as he climbed in behind her, closing the door with one hand while pulling out a gun from a hidden holster under his coat.

"You sit nice and quiet, lady. One chance is all you get."

He waved the gun at her, taunting her to disobey. Blood was stuck to the end of it and Maddie hoped fervently that Jones was going to be okay. She wasn't feeling as optimistic with her own chances of survival. Then she thought of the people who had, and were still suffering at the hands of these two men. Her blood began to boil.

"You know it won't matter where you take me. The sheriff will find you."

Smith laughed as he climbed in the front. "Isn't that sweet that you think so? Far be it from me to dampen your trust in your hero but, as we speak, he's on another wild goose chase."

His continued laughter grated on her nerves as he drove out of the parking lot at a steady speed. At the first intersection Maddie spied a familiar blue Sedan. Chance pushed her head down, rather roughly, so she couldn't be sure if it was Ethan's car or not. She hoped so. But how would he know that she was inside the criminals' vehicle?

She knew Maple Falls inside and out, but the way Smith was driving meant that—despite her best efforts and with her inability to see out the windows—she quickly became disorientated. He must have doubled back through a few country lanes because she couldn't hear any other vehicles.

Smith slowed a little. Managing to turn her head slightly under the large paw, she could see a canopy of trees. The dappled light was receding, but she knew this road. They were headed into the Maple Falls Country Club.

They must have gone around the back because a bump signaled that they had left the drive and were crossing grass. The groundskeeper would have a fit when he saw this tomorrow morning. As soon as she thought it, she bit her lip to remind herself that allowing her mind to wander right now would not be helpful.

They parked and a sensor light came on outside. Smith cursed and jumped out. Smashing glass made her flinch then it was darker once more. Smith yanked her door open and grabbed her arm rather more firmly than was necessary. He half dragged her out of the car and pushed her towards a large shed.

Aside from his deep breathing and the crunch of their shoes on the gravel, it was eerily quiet—as if even the leaves in the trees didn't dare to rustle. Shadows formed around them, and Maddie's heart and mind raced as she sought a way out of this predicament.

Chance was already there, and he unlocked then slid the roller door up to reveal a riding mower and various tools a groundskeeper used. They bypassed this down the right-hand side and went to where a partition separated the back of the shed from one side to the other.

There was no handle on the door, but there was a very large padlock. Smith pulled out another key and unlocked this. Again, she was propelled forward as if she were a doll. It wasn't a big room and looked like it had been made in a rush. There was a small grimy window on the rear wall which barely allowed in any light.

Stacked against the far wall were what looked like large canvases. Beside them was a small table made of a plank of wood held up by small crates. Two canvases sat there, glistening and, after what she'd heard and witnessed, Maddie would bet a whole apple pie that they were either copies or expensive paintings covered in new work.

"Sit down over there." Smith pointed to another slightly larger crate.

"Don't make a move," Chance said through gritted teeth as he hefted a couple of the canvases and went outside.

Smith dragged the others a few at a time to the doorway, using the corners of the cloth that was underneath them. Then Chance took them to the vehicle. They had clearly done this before as they didn't speak. It also meant they didn't intend to leave her alone with any opportunity to escape.

It took a while. There were more paintings than Maddie had thought, making her wonder how they would get them from here to wherever they were going. There was no way they could put all of the stolen art into a car. Therefore, the sedan was out of the question even though it had a large trunk. That must mean there was another vehicle. A van seemed likely, yet she hadn't seen one.

Chance came back to the door, breathing heavily.

"These last few are too heavy and awkward to carry. You'll need to help me with them," he said to Smith.

"Don't even think about moving." Smith glared as he disappeared through the opening.

She heard a vehicle start up ... then another. The second one sounded closer. Creeping to the doorway, she tried to see outside, but the angle was wrong. About to push her luck by following them, she heard footsteps and ran back to the crate.

Smith returned, red-faced and ill-tempered. Physical work did not seem to agree with him. He came so close his feet were barely an inch from hers. He bent down until they were eye to eye.

"I should kill you for sabotaging my plans. Everything was going well until you stuck your nose in where it didn't belong." Then he shrugged, running a finger down her cheek. "Lucky for you, I admire your persistence. And I don't have time to deal with another body. I'm going to lock you in this room. Count yourself lucky I'm not letting my friend deal with you instead. You might be here a few hours, but then again ..."

He smirked and Maddie, sickened by his touch, moved as far back on the crate as she could. His obsidian eyes shone in the glimmer of moonlight from the window, and he looked feral. It seemed like a good idea this once not to say anything, and she looked away but couldn't still her fingers drumming on her thigh.

Her silence clearly annoyed him, as he slammed out of the room without another word. The thin door creaked. Seconds later the lock clicked. She rushed over and pressed her ear to the door, but wasn't able to hear anyone, so she gave it a push, not really expecting it to move, and was surprised when it shook. The little room was poorly built, and even the walls were flimsy.

Was she strong enough to break it down? She didn't think so.

Suddenly she heard the roller door going down. Before it finished there was the sound of a car door slamming ... then two more slams. They had stopped being quiet, but why? Frustrated, she ran to the small window, which was too high to see out of, and looked around her. The crate she had been sitting on would be perfect! She dragged it over to the window and, once she had it in position, she climbed on top of it. The darn thing wobbled, and her arms flailed like a scarecrow in a storm, but luckily it didn't collapse.

From here she had a wide view of the golf course and leaning her face against the window she could also see the front end of a van. A white van! So, there were indeed two vans and Smith and Chance were about to escape in the second one.

She searched for a handle, but this was a window that didn't open. It made sense now, why they had thought she wasn't a threat to them in here. Frantically looking around at the dimly lit room, she spied the crates, planks, and the two paintings.

Smith and Chance had not taken any of the damp art and she couldn't bring herself to be anything but gentle as she lay them on the ground. She picked up the plank, which was a little unwieldy, and hefted it on her shoulder like a javelin then carried it to the window. She leaned back with the wood a couple of feet over her shoulder then rocked backwards and forwards to gain some force.

"One. Two. Three." She leaned one foot forward and hit the glass with everything she had. The cracking sound was its own reward. A couple more whacks and the glass shattered in and out of the shed. Her hands covered her face, but she could feel a few nicks.

The sounds of sirens cut through the quiet of the countryside. Had the crooks heard them too? She took off her jacket and lay it over the jagged glass so that she could lean out. They wouldn't have heard her over the revving of the engines.

Maddie was delighted to hear the wheels skidding in the grass. Great clumps of earth flew into the air, and she knew that the driver of the van had no idea how to get out of the ruts he was forming. She could smell the fumes as the engine strained.

"Help me, you idiot!" Smith screamed at Chance.

The van moved backward and forward as if it were being rocked, but the wheels couldn't find traction. That van wasn't going anywhere in a hurry.

Cursing as the sirens got louder, Smith jumped out, yelling, "We'll both take the car."

"What about the paintings?" Chance roared back.

"Paintings or jail? Your call, but I'm off."

"I'm not leaving empty handed."

"Take the smaller ones, if you must, but do it now, otherwise you're on your own."

This time the cursing came from Chance as she heard the car start up. Not long after, the sedan sped off across the golf course. They had a head start, but it wasn't much. Maddie jumped up and down on the crate as Ethan's car came flying around the trees hot on their heels, followed by two of the deputies' cars. Then they were gone from sight.

Just then, a low moan came from the farthest corner of the room. Maddie jumped off the crate and found an old tarpaulin there. She pulled it back to uncover not one, but two men. One was covered in blood and it was hard to see his face. The other was motionless.

Unfortunately, her phone was back in the car. She remembered that Gran had placed it in the tray beneath the dashboard. So ... no flashlight and no way to call for help. She gave herself a mental slap while she began to check them over.

"I'm sorry Owen. Real sorry," the bloodied man mumbled as he turned to face her.

She couldn't be sure in this light, but he definitely looked familiar. "Mr. Langham? Bertram Langham?"

"Is Owen there? My son?"

She knelt down on the rough cold concrete and felt for his pulse, which was faint. He was in a very bad way. By the cuts on his face, he'd been badly beaten, and blood seeped out through his shirt. A lot of blood. She ripped it open and found a gunshot wound to his chest. She had to get help somehow and soon. She took off her jacket, sweater, and blouse then removed her camisole. Wadding this up, she put it over the wound, then placed his hand firmly on it.

"I'm Madeline Flynn. A friend of Owen's. You have to hold this, Mr. Langham. I'm going to get help."

She said this with a conviction she didn't feel. The only real option was the high window, which entailed a long drop to the ground. Still, the fear of getting hurt wasn't as strong as the fear of watching Owen's father die.

He clutched at her arm. "I remember. Owen's gone. I called you after I collected my cat from Nora's. Your number was beside her phone. I tried to warn you, but Smith found me just as you answered. I'm so sorry for everything. Owen thought a lot of you and your bakery." He gasped in pain as tears trailed down his cheeks.

The call that she'd thought was from Nora had brought

her to this moment, and all along it had been from Owen's father. Maddie placed his fingers back on the wadding.

"Don't talk anymore. Save your strength."

Leaving him, she checked on the other man. He was alive but unresponsive. Her grandfather had taught her to place an unconscious person into the recovery position, but she couldn't think what else to do and time was slipping away. Time that could mean life or death to either of these men.

Covering both of them with the tarpaulin to keep them warm, she put her clothes back on, apart from her cami and jacket. Next, she eased one of the smaller crates out of the window. It hit the grass outside with a soft thump. Then she managed to drop the second one on the first. Next, she used the plank to break off any glass still in the frame of the window. Finally, she put her jacket over the bottom of the frame and, holding her torso up by doing a pull-up on a rough beam in the ceiling, squeezed out the hole feet first.

She hung in the air, not sure how far she had to drop before her feet could touch the crates. Letting go was the hardest part of it, but she took a breath then counted to three again. Her feet hit the crate, but she was too heavy for it and they smashed right through that and the same thing happened with the one underneath.

Now she had two crates around her body that she didn't need. She threw them over her head—heedless of the rough wood that pushed her sleeves up—and ran after the cars, taking a shortcut over the golf course.

Even after she crested the first bunker, not one taillight was visible. They were long gone. She jogged out onto a path that led back to the clubhouse and, after a while, she saw a rainbow in the sky. Blue, white, and red, it seemed to throb. Those colors gave her more hope than anything she could imagine.

Around the last corner she found Ethan. He'd barricaded the exit. The criminals, who had no doubt searched for another way out and failed, had ended up back here just ahead of her.

Smith was revving the sedan's engine as if he might try a game of chicken, but Ethan merely leaned over the hood of his car with a shotgun aimed at them. She couldn't see Ethan's face from here, but his body language looked calm as she slid behind a shrub, well out of the line of fire.

These men didn't know what they had got themselves into with the Sheriff's department of Maple Falls, but Maddie knew Smith and Chance were as cooked as a Thanksgiving Turkey.

Chapter Twenty-Four

Once Smith and Chance were taken into custody, Ethan handed his gun to one of his deputies and ran his hands through his hair, his eyes searching the golf course. Peering through the branches, Maddie finally felt safe enough to show herself.

He saw her immediately and emitted an anguished sound as he ran to meet her in the middle of the parking lot.

"You couldn't sit at home and do nothing, could you?" he said gruffly as he pulled her to him.

She could have stayed there forever, but there were other people to think about.

"Bertram Langham is in the groundskeeper's shed. He and another man are hurt really bad and need an ambulance."

Ethan leaned back, shook his head at her, then yelled over his shoulder, "Rob get an ambulance here, ASAP."

She pulled on his arm. "I'll show you the shortcut."

"Don't you want to stay here where it's safe?"

"Are you kidding me? I don't want to be anywhere near

those two." She snuggled into his chest again with a shiver. She sensed rather than saw his smile.

"Then Rob's coming too, just in case these two aren't working alone." He signaled to his deputy.

Rob had made the call and now the three of them jumped in the front of Ethan's car and raced back to the shed with Maddie pointing out the way she'd come. It was quite a distance and the car wasn't built for this terrain, but they got there in one piece.

Without preamble, Rob shot the lock off the roller door and raced inside. Between the two of them, they wrestled the internal door off its hinges. By this time, they could hear the ambulance. Rob went outside to wave them down while Maddie and Ethan checked on Langham and the other man, who was still unconscious.

Langham was hanging in there, but only just. Maddie held his hand, while Ethan checked the room. He came to kneel beside them and spoke softly to the older man.

"Mr. Langham. Can you tell me what Smith and Chance were going to do with all these paintings?"

"I'm sorry," Langham murmured then moaned.

"Shhh. It's okay." Maddie tried to calm his agitation by patting his arm.

The ambulance arrived and the paramedics were ushered in by Rob. Maddie and Ethan eased out of the confined space and waited outside the roller door.

When she shivered, Ethan put his jacket around her shoulders. She smiled then frowned.

"He kept saying that ... about Owen ... that he was sorry. The two must have met several times to have developed a bond so quickly."

Ethan nodded. "They met many times."

Her eyes widened. "You knew they were related all along?"

He gave a crooked grin. "Not from the beginning. Careful questioning of people like Mavis and Nora can prove very helpful. They know everything that happens in the retirement community. Even if they don't know what it all means. You just have to ask the right questions."

Bertram was brought out on a gurney and placed in the ambulance, then they did the same for the other man. In the brighter light, they could see who it was.

"The groundskeeper," Ethan stated.

"It will be interesting to see how much he knows. If he makes it," Rob said.

"He's in a bad way, isn't he?"

"I'm afraid so," Ethan concurred.

"I'm not sure if he's guilty or innocent, but he had to know about the room at the back of his shed."

"That's true." Ethan led the way to Rob's car.

"I need to follow them to see how he does and speak to him if I get the opportunity. His testimony will help keep the other two behind bars for a long while. I can drop you two at the station on the way."

She sat in the back—eyes closed while she tried to assimilate the day. Then she gasped, "What about Detective Jones? Is he okay?"

"Luckily, he only has a bad concussion, but luckier still not to have drowned. With you to worry about, I guess they weren't as thorough as they could have been."

Rob covered his laugh with a cough.

She ignored them both as Ethan dropped Rob off by the clubhouse to pick up his car.

"Was that you I saw at the end of the road by the retirement community, Ethan?" she asked when they were on their way again.

"It was. I wanted to follow their car, but I knew Steve was around there somewhere and the fact he wasn't close on their heels meant I had to find him when he didn't answer my calls. Rob was already questioning residents when I found him."

"I bet he's going to be mad at me."

"I can't think why."

This time they both laughed. Perhaps she should be offended, but what was the point when they were right?

"Okay, now that you've made fun of me, you can catch me up on what I don't know. Please."

Ethan groaned, but nodded. "You'd better come to the hospital with me. Maybe he'll be awake and can fill in the blanks that we haven't managed yet."

Maddie sat back and allowed herself a small smile. She wouldn't mind hearing the whole story, and she wanted more than anything for there to be a happy ending for Owen's dad. If only for the fact that she hated to think his death had been for nothing.

When Ethan saw her in the light, he made a rude noise.

"You're hurt."

She shrugged, although her body protested with the slight movement. "Just a few scrapes."

"You are not going anywhere until you've been thoroughly checked out."

She knew that stubborn look and had little energy to argue, so she allowed herself to be poked and prodded by a nurse. Disinfectant hurt like a swarm of bees, and her teeth ached from being gritted for so long, but there was no serious damage.

"I told you, I'm fine."

He raised an eyebrow and scoffed. "Fine, as we all know, is not a word to be accepted at face value from a woman."

"Pardon?" Her eyebrows had talents of their own.

Ethan decided not to pursue the matter. "I'm glad you're okay. Now I've got to get to Langham."

"Let's go then." She picked up her jacket she'd rescued from the window back at the shed, but didn't put it on, since there were potentially a few splinters of glass still embedded in the sleeves.

He brushed the hair from her face and, with a warm smile proving once more that his annoyance and frustration were driven by his feelings for her, led her down the corridor of the small hospital.

The deputy posted nearby informed them that Langham had not spoken and was in surgery. At this stage, loss of blood was the main issue as the wound had missed important organs and veins. It sounded positive, so after calling Gran with a brief synopsis, Maddie curled herself into a ball on a wooden bench and stayed that way while Ethan visited Detective Jones.

She hadn't realized she'd nodded off until Ethan's hand touched her shoulder.

"Come on, sleeping beauty. Time for home."

Maddie took his outstretched hand. "I can't believe I slept."

"Exhaustion and stress will do that to a person. Besides, you look darned cute, even with all the cuts."

"I just bet." She laughed ruefully, which sounded too loud in the quiet hall. More softly she asked, "Is Langham out of surgery?"

"He is. I've spoken to him for as long as the doctor

would allow, but I believe I have most of the story. His version of it, at least."

"What about the groundskeeper? He was new, wasn't he?"

"Was that a guess?"

"A supposition."

"A darned good one. How'd you get to it?"

"1. The person who made that room did it especially for these crimes, because it was flimsy and not built to last. 2. Security wasn't a problem, because that roller door was strong and always locked. 3. If he was new in town, he wouldn't know a lot of people, so he wouldn't have unwanted visitors. And 4. The groundskeeper wasn't the one complaining about his golf course which doesn't make sense because everyone knows there's a pride associated with a perfect green."

Ethan shook his head in wonder. "Precisely. He's either very disoriented or putting on a good act, but we'll make sure he isn't going anywhere."

With their fingers still entwined, they went outside. She was glad of the fresh air after the stuffiness of the hospital and eager for more details. This sleuthing business was a lot like baking. Each new recipe meant failing a few times but, in the end, you understood what ingredients or clues made it finally come together. In both cases, all she wanted was a happy outcome, but how could that be when someone innocent had died?

Ethan made sure she was comfortable then pulled out of the parking lot. Usually she was the one tapping something, so when his fingers drummed the wheel, she could tell he had something on his mind.

"Are you still worried about the case?" She pointed to his fingers.

"Looks like I'm picking up one of your habits. I'm hoping you aren't picking up too many of mine."

"Are you still mad at me for going to the retirement community when I said I wouldn't?"

"I wish it was that. I was scared. Plain and simple. The thought of losing you again is always at the back of my mind. I knew that Smith and Chance had no trouble killing. Not knowing if you had been taken by them was sickening and frustrating. I'm usually totally focused when I'm on a case, but with you involved I'm not convinced I'm as effective as I need to be."

Maddie's chin sank to her chest. "You're a wonderful sheriff, and the last thing I want is for you to doubt your ability to do your job because of me. I honestly don't go looking for trouble. It just seems to find its way to Maple Lane Bakery." She put her hands out. "And I like to think I have helped in some way."

He was silent.

"Do you want me to promise to keep out of your way?"

Unbelievably, he snorted, and she raised her head to see his wry grin.

"Maddie, the truth is that you have a need to help people, just like your Gran. I get it. Just don't expect me to be happy when it endangers you."

"You mean that as much as it bothers you, you'll put up with me?"

He pulled up at the corner of Maple Lane and turned to face her. "I have no choice. I love you."

She gasped.

He frowned. "Is that so terrible?"

She shook her head, her fingers clenched together.

"Unexpected?"

What was she supposed to say? He put on the light and

watched her fight her fears. She reached up and switched it off, preferring to do her heart wrangling in semidarkness.

Ethan sighed then drove around the corner of the bakery to the apartment.

All the lights were burning, and she appreciated her family and friends would need to know she was okay. Her phone was still in Honey at the retirement community and would have to stay there until tomorrow since she couldn't entertain the thought of driving tonight. But the call to Gran from the hospital was never going to be enough. There was no possibility of her getting to bed any time soon.

Ethan came around the car and helped her out. He pulled her into his arms, and she went willingly, under-standing he was still waiting for a clearer response to his declaration of love. He kissed her. At first it was incredibly gentle. Then it morphed into a passion so strong it took her breath away. On and on it went until her knees began to weaken.

He pulled back. "Get inside before I whisk you away. Even if you don't feel the same as I do."

He was smiling again and at that precise moment her heart overflowed like a punctured lava cake.

"Why, Sheriff, I didn't think this was a mystery you needed help solving. But you seem to have missed the obvious clues. As it happens, I do love you. Very much."

His eyes widened. Letting out a yell, he picked her up and smashed his lips onto hers. The kitchen door opened, and several faces appeared at the window. He put her down and gave her a gorgeous grin, flashing that dimple she loved.

"It's been a long day, and it looks like you'll be having a long night. As much as I want to stay with you, I need sleep too. I'll see you tomorrow though."

"After that kiss, you'd better," she teased.

He kissed her once more, tenderly, then she floated up the walk as he drove off, her fingers touching swollen lips. This had started out as one crazy relationship and morphed into something that was better than anything she had experienced. It felt like this was the first time she had truly loved a man. Including a much younger Ethan Tanner.

Chapter Twenty-Five

The Girlz glanced at each other across the counter then back to Gran, who had called them to her like chicks to a hen. Big Red was giving her his displeased look until Maddie bent down to pick him up. He lay precariously on her lap because his bulk was that much bigger, but he was content to perch on the seat with her. Rubbing her face in the reassuring softness of his body she looked over the top of him.

"I still don't get why you're all here at this time of night."

Gran bristled. "After what I witnessed at Sunny Days and what you told me, I didn't care to wonder about everyone's safety any longer. The only way to assuage my concern was to have them be where I can see them. Then I could just concentrate on worrying about you. And Ethan."

Maddie grimaced. "Sorry. Things didn't pan out the way I thought they would when I left you."

"That is an understatement, sweetheart." Gran sniffed.

The others sat quietly, waiting for the post-mortem of the case. Maddie had heard it from Ethan. Now it was time to pass it on. She was sore, tired, and dirty, but the Girlz placed a cup of English Breakfast tea—her favorite—and a slice of Gran's chocolate cake in front of her, so it wasn't all bad. First, she needed a long sip of the tea. Gran began to check her scrapes even though Maddie explained that a nurse already had.

Suzy was the least patient, which was to be expected when she had a vested interest with her mother being involved. "So, Owen found out about Bertram Langham being his father and he came to Maple Falls to get him to go straight?"

"According to Bertram, Owen found out about his father living here by accident. He was doing a delivery and saw his father outside the gallery. I can vouch for the fact that the two men look very much alike."

"I can too." Mavis was nursing her teacup sitting in a chair at the table. She had looked shell-shocked on Maddie's arrival and didn't look much better now.

Gran went to sit beside her. "Drink up Mavis. A cup of tea will bring some color to your cheeks."

"I feel so bad that I let that Mr. Smith into my home when he could have killed Maddie or that lovely Detective Jones."

"Shush. No one holds you responsible. He was a clever man. You weren't to know that he wasn't who he said he was."

"Or Bertram. How could he have been caught up in this? He had a son that he never saw, but he was so sweet to everyone here. He helped us with anything we couldn't manage. Even Nora." Mavis finished speaking with a hiccup.

"Mr. Langham didn't want to be found, even by his son. He was ashamed of his former life. And no one would have made the connection, especially when Bertram never mentioned having a child. They even had different names, because Owen had been adopted by his stepfather."

Gran shook her head. "I like to think I know most of the population of Maple Falls, but I hardly knew him at all. Considering how much time I spend at Sunny Days or with people from there, it should have been a clue that something was amiss."

"It is odd that we all knew Owen who had only been coming to town for several months, but a man who'd lived here for several years was a stranger," Angel said with sadness.

"Carry on Maddie," Suzy pressed.

"Against his will, Owen's father got himself mixed up with Smith and Chance in the last year. Having done time for theft before, he'd moved here to lie low and stay out of trouble, but someone recognized him. He was threatened with exposure. When that didn't work, they threatened his family. I should say ex-family."

"So, he was actually protecting Owen and his mom?" Angel's eyes grew misty.

"Exactly. And no matter that he hadn't seen his son for years, he couldn't let him get hurt. Especially when they had only just found each other. At first, it was just pinching jewelry and things that might go unnoticed for some time from the country club members, but that wasn't enough for Smith."

"That's when the painting forgery began?" Suzy asked.

"It was actually an insurance scam that Smith had devised in other states. It was lucrative, because people didn't realize that the paintings were swapped, so they never reported them stolen. The key was to never stay too long in one place."

Laura frowned. "But why Maple Falls?"

"Because they heard of Nicholas Brack and his problems from Bertram. Smith also saw inside one of the retirement community's apartments, and he found another cash cow. Plus ... the gallery, with only Suzy's mom in attendance most days. It was easy pickings and a way to hide paintings until they could ship them."

"So, Owen found out about it, how?"

"Apparently, he overheard them talking about milking the place then using his father as the scapegoat."

"That must have been why he was hanging around the gallery and Sunny Days so much. Owen was trying to stop the thefts. Poor boy." Gran was holding Angel's hand.

Laura nodded. "True. It's just a shame he didn't speak to Ethan or Rob, since he clearly wasn't very good at playing detective."

Maddie agreed with Laura's sadly accurate statement. "Having recently found his father, Owen wasn't prepared to lose him. Shocked though he may have been to learn of his father's activities, he took it upon himself to find out as much as he could about the operation, but like you said, Laura, he was too obvious."

"Obvious enough that Mr. Clayton noticed Owen lurking near the Gallery and probably told others." Laura grimaced.

"Still, his father stepped in to save Nicholas Brack from being killed. Hopefully, that will help his case." Angel tapped a pink tipped finger on the counter.

"He's suffering with the loss of his only child, even if he never really knew him. I hope the law goes a little easy on him."

"But Gran, he was a thief."

"Yes, Suzy, he was. He'll have to live with all that. Just

like Nicholas will have to pay for all the fraud he committed."

"How did he get involved?" Suzy asked.

"Nicholas and Bertram were friends. Perhaps the only true friends each other had. Smith found out that Nicholas had terrible debts, and that was all he needed to force him into forgery. Aside from paying his debts, Nicholas was distraught about having to sell his favorite painting that his late wife had done of the two of them. It was the large one missing from the wall of the gallery. At his request, Cora had taken it down and was holding it for him until he had all the money he needed to buy it back."

"Of course. That makes sense. He had been in and out of the gallery for the last few months and had every opportunity to swap his forgeries for the real ones if Mom was busy with other clients or she was out back. I should have thought about him earlier." Suzy berated herself.

"None of us picked up on it. You know, I think that's all I can manage until after I eat this cake." Maddie took a large bite, hoping a bit of sugar would give her the energy to last a little longer. Then she would have to get in a hot bath or seize up completely.

"Is Detective Jones going to be okay?" Angel asked casually.

Maddie wiped her mouth. "Sorry, I meant to say that although he's concussed, Ethan said he'll be fine. He also told Ethan to apologize on his behalf for not accepting our help. Apparently, we aren't so bad at sleuthing as he thought."

"I knew he was only acting gruff, because that's how people expect a detective to be. He doesn't have family here, so perhaps we should visit him?"

Gran snorted. "He'll be happy to see you, Angel. No need to have us all there exhausting the poor man."

Maddie hid a smile. Angel was never going to be great at keeping secrets, and the fact that she was a little smitten with the tall fair detective was as obvious as the lack of gloss on untempered chocolate.

Laura had a dreamy look on her face too. Was Gran working some sort of magic? Or was it simply time that they all moved on from the band of four? Maddie would hate to see that happen.

Gran wasn't done. "Things worked out okay. We don't need to have a celebration, since not everyone came out of this well, but let's have a quiet meal and a drink tomorrow night at the cottage?"

"Just us?" Laura asked.

"I think so. All your men can come see you another time. Let's just be the Girlz? You can be an honorary one for the night, Mavis."

The women blustered that they had no men in their lives—all except Maddie. Now that they had professed their love, spending time with Ethan was a serious consideration. But she would be happy to make time for these women who were so important to her.

And Maple Falls was safe once more.

Thanks so much for reading Cookies and Chaos. I hope you enjoyed it!

If you did...

1 Help other people find this book by leaving a review.

2 Sign up for my new release e-mail, so you can find out about the next book as soon as it's available.

3 Come like my Facebook page.

4 Visit my website for the very best deals.

5 Keep reading for an excerpt from Doughnuts and Disaster.

Doughnuts and Disaster

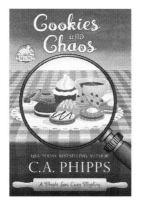

They walked for twenty minutes, with Suzy keeping her good-natured moans to a minimum. Angel fell in love with the outdoors ever since she moved to Maple Falls as a young girl, while Laura was a complete stranger to it.

Maddie enjoyed their wonder and stopped often to answer questions about names and varieties of plants as well as species of birds and small animals.

"Thanks so much for inviting me. I never would have

ventured this far from town on my own," Laura admitted when they stopped to watch a small owl who looked at them from half-closed lids. "What's his name?"

"That's a Northern saw-whet owl, one of the most common forest owls in Oregon. They grow approximately eight inches in height. They're shy, so it's rare to see one."

"He's a cutie." Suzy showed that she wasn't totally immune to nature.

"The white V above his eyes makes him look majestic," Angel noted.

Maddie was about to comment further when a rifle shot rang out. She swung in the general direction, listening intently. *Was that someone yelling?*

"Stay here," she commanded. The other women had looked to her for reassurance and weren't happy about her leaving, but there was no choice if someone was in trouble, and she was the fastest.

Perhaps a gun went off accidentally, she thought as she ran towards muted sounds of cussing.

Leaping over shrubs and foliage, Maddie arrived at the edge of a clearing as fast as she could. The thought occurred to her that the noise she was making wasn't conducive to a stealthy approach. On the far side stood Bernie's cabin and halfway between it and her hiding place lay a man, face down in the dirt. Blood seeped into the ground around him.

She ducked behind a shrub, not sure what to do. Was this an accident? If it were then the rifle would be visible, and it wasn't. He could be lying on it, but she doubted a part of it wouldn't be protruding.

Then, from behind the cabin, she heard the sound of running footsteps pounding on dirt and heading away from her. A car door slammed, followed by the start of an engine.

Its tires sounded as though they were spinning, trying to find traction in the gravel, and then the engine noise faded.

Waiting several, anxious seconds more, she chanced another look. Scanning the circle of forest and the cabin, which was about twenty feet from her. This cabin was older and a lot smaller than Grandad's. She'd passed this way often on the many hikes she'd taken with him. Bernie had sometimes been here, and if he were, they'd taken time to visit.

All was quiet. She stepped quietly out from behind the shrub in a runner's pose, unsure how many people had been here. But Maddie was determined to try to help. If the man was only wounded, and she hoped that the situations wasn't worse, he would need assistance as soon as possible.

Running low to the ground, she approached the body. A key lay on the ground, close to one hand as if he'd managed to pull it from his pocket only to drop it from his lifeless fingers as he fell. A circle of red, as wide as her two hands, covered the back of his plaid shirt, which had a rip along the bottom of it. And the pool of blood was ever-widening. His head was turned to face her, eyes wide.

Maddie knelt closer and checked for a pulse. It was the one thing a person did, Ethan had told her, even when they knew, as in this case, that it was too late. She plucked her phone from her coat pocket and tried to call him.

Reception faded in and out, and she had to stand holding her phone out and up in the air to get one bar. It went to voicemail, so she dialed 911. Frustratingly, it took several attempts, but finally she managed to give her location, name, and number in a rush before losing connection completely. She hoped whoever had been on the other end of the line had heard her.

The air felt damp, and although the lake couldn't be

seen through the trees, the sound of small waves lapping at the shore was faintly audible. In the distance, the mountains rose with their dusting of snow—the beauty was in direct contrast to the crime that had just occurred.

A noise of something falling in the cabin made her spin around. She stood and walked slowly towards it. She'd heard a car leave, so surely the perpetrator wouldn't still be here. Unless they had snuck back? Or there were more than one? She moved to the cabin wall, her vivid imagination expecting to see a gun pointed at her on the other side of the window that faced the small deck. No one appeared.

Smash!

Maddie wished she'd picked up the axe she'd noticed not far from the body. Since there was no way of knowing if someone was hiding inside, and not wanting to be caught out in the open if there was, Maddie crept around to the back of the cabin—heart racing, palms sweaty.

A window was open. In a crouch, Maddie made her way underneath it, then stood on a piece of firewood to peer over the sill into the only room. The place looked empty. It was tidy, apart from an overturned chair and a box of cereal spilled across the kitchen counter.

She was contemplating climbing in when a noise that was too close for comfort startled her, making her lose her balance. The log rolled from under her, and she went down, arms flailing, to land in a heap on the bare ground.

Need to read more?
Pick up your copy of Doughnuts and Disaster today!

Recipes

These recipes are ones I use all the time and have come down the generations from my mum, grandmother, and some I have adapted from other recipes. Also, I now have my husband's grandmother's recipe book. Exciting! I'll be bringing some of them to life very soon.

Just a wee reminder, that I am a New Zealander. Occasionally I may have missed converting into ounces and pounds for my American readers.

My apologies for that, and please let me know—if you do try them—how they turn out.

Cheryl x

Chocolate Croissants

Ingredients

Makes 8 servings

4 cups flour (500 g)

½ cup water (120 mL)

½ cup milk (120 mL)

¼ cup sugar (50 g)

2 teaspoons salt

1 packet instant dry yeast

3 tablespoons unsalted butter, softened

1 ¼ cups cold unsalted butter, cut into ½-inch (1 cm) thick slices (285 g)

1 egg, beaten

2 bars 70% cocoa chocolate

Instructions

1 In a large bowl, mix the flour, water, milk, sugar, salt, yeast, and butter.

2 Once the dough starts to clump, turn it out onto a clean counter.

3 Lightly knead the dough and form it into a ball, making sure not to over-knead it.

4 Cover the dough with plastic wrap and refrigerate for one hour.

5 Slice the cold butter in thirds and place it onto a sheet of parchment paper.

6 Place another piece of parchment on top of the butter and beat it with a rolling pin.

7 Keeping the parchment paper on the butter, use a rolling pin to roll the butter into a 7-inch (18 cm) square, ½-inch (1 cm) thick. If necessary, use a knife to trim the edges and place the trimmings back on top of the butter and continue to roll into a square.

8 Transfer the butter layer to the refrigerator.

10 To roll out the dough, lightly flour the counter. Place the dough on the counter, and push the rolling pin once vertically into the dough and once horizontally to form four quadrants.

11 Roll out each corner and form a 10-inch (25 cm) square.

12 Place the butter layer on top of the dough and fold the sides of the dough over the butter, enclosing it completely.

13 Roll the dough with a rolling pin to seal the seams, making sure to lengthen the dough, rather than widening it.

14 Transfer the dough to a baking sheet and cover with plastic wrap. Refrigerate for 1 hour.

15 Roll out the dough on a floured surface until it's 8x24 inches (20x61 cm).

16 Fold the top half down to the middle, and brush off any excess flour.

17 Fold the bottom half over the top and turn the dough clockwise to the left. This completes the first turn.

18 Cover and refrigerate for one hour.

19 Roll out the dough again two more times, completing

three turns in total and refrigerating for 1 hour in between each turn. If at any time the dough or butter begins to soften, stop and transfer back to the fridge.

20 After the final turn, cover the dough with plastic wrap and refrigerate overnight.

21 To form the croissants, cut the dough in half. Place one half in the refrigerator.

22 Flour the surface and roll out the dough into a long narrow strip, about 8x40 inches (20x101 cm).

23 With a knife, trim the edges of the dough.

24 Cut the dough into 4 rectangles.

25 Place the chocolate on the edge of the dough and roll tightly enclosing it in the dough.

26 Place the croissants on a baking sheet, seam side down.

27 Repeat with the other half of the dough.

28 Brush the croissants with the beaten egg. Save the rest of the egg wash in the fridge for later.

29 Place the croissants in a warm place to rise for 1-2 hours.

30 Preheat oven to 400°F (200°C).

31 Once the croissants have proofed, brush them with one more layer of egg wash.

32 Bake for 15 minutes or until golden brown and cooked through. Serve warm.

Enjoy!

If the recipe above gave you the horrors, how about trying this quicker version on the next page?

Cheats Croissant

(Just as good!)

Ingredients

1 packet of pre-made flaky pastry sheets.

1 block of dark chocolate – I use a 70% cocoa one.

A little milk

Instructions:

1 Preheat oven to 400°F (200°C).

2 Cut each sheet of pastry into quarters then halve each quarter to give you 8 triangles.

3 Place the chocolate on the long end of the pastry and roll away from you. Twist the ends to form that horned croissant look.

4 Brush with milk

5 Bake for 15 minutes or until golden brown and cooked through. Serve warm.

Chocolate Truffles

Ingredients

3 ½ ounces (100g) unsalted butter

3 ½ ounces (100g) 70% cocoa chocolate

1 cup icing sugar

1 Tbsp rum

1 tsp cocoa

fine desiccated or shredded coconut

chocolate hail

Instructions

1 Put the butter and chocolate into a saucepan and heat gently, stirring until melted.

2 Add ½ cup of the icing sugar and stir until the mixture is thick

3 Add the rum and cocoa.

4 Add the remaining icing sugar to form a stiff dough.

5 Using a tablespoonful scoop out the mixture and shape into balls.

6 Roll in the coconut or chocolate hail and chill until firm.

Chocolate Chip Cookies

Ingredients

225g (1 cup) caster sugar

300g (2 cups) plain flour (sifted)

200g (1 cup) of butter melted

1 tsp vanilla extract

1 tsp of baking powder

A pinch of salt

1 egg

100g-200g chocolate bar or chocolate chips

Instructions

1 Add the sugar and melted butter in a bowl and mix together – a wooden spoon is fine, no need for a whisk.

2 Sift the flour, baking powder, vanilla and salt together and add to the sugar and butter mixture. Add the chocolate chips at this stage if you're making chocolate chip cookies.

3 Mix together using your hand. Once you get a dough texture, add the egg and knead using your hand again.

4 Spread some butter onto a baking tray. Take some of the dough, roll into ball then flatten a little. Keep them on the

small side as they spread out during baking. Also, don't keep biscuits close to each other otherwise they will get stuck together.

5 Place in the oven and bake at 160C, 320F for 10-20 mins.

The bigger the cookies, the longer they'll take to cook. They're ready when the edges are golden.

Mini Fruit Tarts

Ingredients

2 cups of milk

2 tbsp vanilla essence

¾ cups of sugar

6 large egg yolks

3 tbsp cornstarch

½ tsp salt

7 oz (200g) of butter

1 packet of sweet short pastry (4 sheets)

Any berries in season

Instructions

1 Mix milk and vanilla essence in a pot and bring to the boil.

2 In a bowl at sugar to the egg yolks. Whisk until egg yolks have lightened in color.

3 Add 3 tbsp cornstarch and ½ tsp salt and whisk.

4 Slowly add the hot milk a little at a time so that the egg doesn't curdle.

5 Put back into saucepan and place over a medium heat.

6 Bring it to the boil while whisking constantly until the custard thickens.

7 After a few minutes remove from heat and add 200g of butter a little at a time, whisking until smooth and it all has been added.

8 Cover for a couple of hours or leave overnight so that it sets.

9 Cut pastry sheets and place in non-stick mini pans.

10 Place baking paper and then rice or cooking beans in each one.

11 Cook for 8-10 minutes or until brown.

12 Cool.

13 Mix the custard until smooth again and fill the pastry cases.

14 Decorate with lovely ripe berries or kiwifruit. 😋

Also by C. A. Phipps

Midlife Potions - Paranormal Cozy Mysteries

Witchy Awakening

Witchy Hot Spells

Witchy Flash Back

Witchy Bad Blood - preorder now!

The Cozy Café Mysteries

Sweet Saboteur

Candy Corruption

Mocha Mayhem

Berry Betrayal

Deadly Double-Dip

The Maple Lane Cozy Mysteries

Sugar and Sliced - Maple Lane Prequel

Apple Pie and Arsenic

Bagels and Blackmail

Cookies and Chaos

Doughnuts and Disaster

Eclairs and Extortion

Fudge and Frenemies

Gingerbread and Gunshots

Honey Cake and Homicide - preorder now!

Beagle Diner Cozy Mysteries

Beagles Love Cupcake Crimes

Beagles Love Steak Secrets

Beagles Love Muffin But Murder

Beagles Love Layer Cake Lies - preorder now!

Please note: Most are also available in paperback and some in audio.

Remember to join Cheryl's Cozy Mystery newsletter.

There's a free recipe book waiting for you. ;-)

Cheryl also writes romance as Cheryl Phipps.

About the Author

'Life is a mystery. Let's follow the clues together.'

C. A. Phipps is a USA Today best-selling author from beautiful New Zealand. Cheryl lives in a quiet suburb with her wonderful husband, whom she married the moment she left school (yes, they were high school sweethearts). With three married children and seven grandchildren to keep her busy when she's not writing, there is just enough space for a crazy mixed breed dog who stole her heart! She enjoys family times, baking, rambling walks, and her quest for the perfect latte.

Check out her website http://caphipps.com

facebook.com/authorcaphipps
x.com/CherylAPhipps
instagram.com/caphippsauthor

Made in the USA
Middletown, DE
18 August 2024